Dirty Love

Broken Boys, Volume 2

Zane Menzy

Published by Zane Menzy, 2023.

This is a work of fiction. Similarities to real people, places, or events are entirely coincidental.

DIRTY LOVE

First edition. October 23, 2023.

ISBN: 979-8223739227

Written by Zane Menzy.

Chapter 1

I FLICKED MY GAZE BACK to the red screen and watched distractedly as bullets rained through my body. Barely glancing at the file of my mission results, I slid my thumb downwards, pressing to continue. Back from the dead, I cocked my gun and raised it as I stealthily scanned the tunnel, and charged ahead for the fifth time in an hour. Minutes later and I faced the same viscous, red liquid dripping down his screen. I tossed the controller onto the couch beside me and sank back into the cushions. There was no point. I hadn't been able to focus on anything since I'd woken up an hour ago to rid myself of Jockey's seed.

The noises my ass had made on the toilet were mortifying, the hisses and splutters leaving no doubt as to what my body had endured last night. I still couldn't believe what I'd done—let myself get fucked by Jockey Savage. My asshole was still tender from our romp at the beach and each time it throbbed I felt myself blush with shame. The funny thing was it wasn't so much the fact I'd lost my virginity to another male that bothered me. It was because of who that male was and the position I'd been in. Whenever I had fantasized about being with a bloke, I'd always been the dominant. The one doing the fucking. But that wasn't what had happened last night. I'd been on the receiving end of another man's lust. A man—if you could call him that—who in many regards was lower down the pecking order.

In the immediate aftermath of losing my virginity I'd been floating, wondering when we could do it again. Now though, with the benefit of hindsight and being sober, I wanted nothing more than to forget last night had ever happened. It had been a mistake. A terrible mistake. Jockey hadn't even waited two minutes before getting dressed and telling me he was going to walk home. That meant I was left there on my own, too drunk to drive. I'd had to go sit in Gavin's car for nearly two hours by myself before I felt sober enough to drive home—even then I'm sure I was still over the limit.

To my surprise, Jockey hadn't text me yet. It wasn't like he text me every single day but considering the events of last night I had thought he may have reached out today at some point, even if it were just to say thank you again. I mean, I'd gifted the wannabe soldier something no one else would ever get—my virginity.

I thought about Jockey and the way his body had felt upon my own. I thought about him with his smug grin as he told me to "take it like a man" and how afterward, his come dripping down my thighs, he had got dressed and left me there at the beach. And although I could feel a hard-on coming on and excitedly ran my hand down between my legs, I felt, at the same time, a cold, humiliated fury at my second-best friend and at the world.

Deciding that killing shit wasn't helping me forget the dull ache in my ass, I ditched the Xbox and made my way into the kitchen to finally make myself some breakfast. I'd barely sat down with my bowl of cornflakes when the sound of footsteps approached the kitchen. I looked over and spotted inky black hair atop of a face that looked almost as tired as mine. It was Gavin. He staggered into the kitchen, hand inside his baggy boxers as he scratched his furry balls before making his way to the kettle. The sight of Gavin half-naked didn't usually bother me but considering my recent acceptance into the cocksuckers club the last thing I needed right now was to see a man molesting his junk.

"What time did you get in last night?" he asked as he stifled a yawn.

"Late."

"Must've been. I didn't head to bed until nearly two am and you still weren't back."

"It was Jockey's birthday so I was sort of obliged to stay late."

"That's right. How was it?"

"Good."

"Just good?" Gavin began smirking. "From where I'm standing it looks like you had more than just a good night."

How did he know? It wasn't as if he had psychic powers that could sense a fucked asshole.

"I don't know what you're talking about," I said defensively.

He walked over, still smirking, and rubbed the side of my neck. "I'm talking about all this root rash you going on. Whoever she was she must have some big fucking teeth."

"What?" I rubbed the spot he'd just touched. "I have hickeys?"

"Both sides by the looks of it." He leaned forward and peered down my shirt. "And they look like they go right down."

I rushed to the bathroom in search of a mirror. "Oh fuck," I muttered when I saw my reflection. My neck was absolutely covered in bright purple marks. I lifted my shirt and saw there were more on my chest, mostly around my nipples. *That horny fucker!* I was mad. So fucking mad. How did I not realise he'd marked me like a dog's chew toy.

How fucking drunk was I last night?

When I returned to the kitchen, Gavin was sat at the table with his coffee. The juvenile smirk still on his face. "Like I said, must have been a good night. Especially if you don't remember getting them."

"I remember," I grumbled as I returned to my bowl of cornflakes. "I just forgot."

"You don't sound pleased. Was she a mutt?"

"No comment."

"No judgement here, buddy. I've had my fair share of munters." He took a sip on his coffee before continuing a conversation I didn't want to have. "I just hoped you used a raincoat. Don't want you ending up a teenage parent."

"What?"

"A condom. You used one, right?"

"Just because a guy has hickeys doesn't mean he had sex."

"No, but judging how low down some of them teeth marks go I'm picking shit got pretty hot and heavy last night." He leaned over and sniffed. "Not to mention you've got that morning after sex smell going on."

"A morning after sex smell?" My voice cracked.

"You know. All sweaty and stale. Like a gym locker but with more spunk."

I willed a sinkhole to open up beneath my chair and swallow me whole.

"Now I'm an easy-going sort of dude," Gavin continued, "but if you gonna screw around then just make sure you do it safe. We can barely afford to feed ourselves without adding child maintenance to the bills."

"Trust me, Gavin. No one got pregnant last night."

"That's good. But just make sure you play safe, okay?"

I gave him a frosty nod then shovelled in a spoonful of cornflakes.

Thankfully Gavin got the hint I didn't want to discuss last night's hickey-fest anymore. Instead, he started nattering about the good weather we were having and then about the new Kmart that was opening up in town. Safe and mundane topics I was happy to nod my way through without fear of exposing myself as the new owner of a fucked asshole.

Done with breakfast, I went and put my bowl in the sink, now desperate to take a shower and wash away the morning after sex smell Gavin said he could smell on me. Just before I left the room though, Gavin called out. "Hey, Mikey..."

"Yeah?"

"Congratulations," he said with a wink.

I knew what he meant. And as cringe as it was I knew he meant well. "Thanks, Gavin."

"And don't worry. It gets better. The first time is always a bit messy."

And on that understatement of the century, I went to go wash my no longer virgin body.

Chapter 2

GAVIN WAS CURLED UP on his side, watching a rugby match on the sports channel, knees pulled up to make room for me at the other end, while his feet rested against my thigh. Such close proximity didn't usually bother me but after what had happened with Jockey I found the touch of Gavin's pale feet both irritating and unnerving. Yet at the same time I wanted to be near him.

I don't know why but ever since I'd been a child, and if I were upset about something, I liked to be near Gavin. It could have been grazing my knee, getting in trouble at school, or a fallout with a work colleague, I'd always found the man's presence soothing. His laidback vibe was a safety blanket I wanted to cuddle into, and after the week I'd been having his presence was most needed.

I'd just walked in the door ten minutes before from an eight-hour shift at the cafe, and had collapsed beside him on the couch. My feet were sore as fuck. I didn't usually work a full day but I had asked Carol for extra hours and she'd kindly supplied them. Part of the reason for the extra hours was I wanted the cash, but it was also to keep myself busy so I wouldn't keep obsessing over things I shouldn't be obsessing about. Working full-time hours was taking some getting used to though. Not only were my feet aching more than usual but I'd sweated like a pig each shift courtesy of the turtleneck sweater I'd had to wear to cover up those damn hickeys. It had been six days since I'd first woken up with a neck resembling that of a Dalmatian and the hickeys had finally almost faded to nothing; I figured that tomorrow I could go to work in a t-shirt. Thank fuck.

With one eye on the game and the other on my phone, I checked for any new messages. There weren't any. He still hadn't messaged me. The *he* in question wasn't Brian for a change—although he'd yet to make contact either—it was Jockey.

Despite a week having almost past since the trashy stoner had fucked me, I still hadn't heard a peep from the cherry-popping bastard. No, 'thank you.' No, 'I had a great time.' No, 'Did you enjoy your first time?' None of that, of course none of that. What was most infuriating was I'd never waited for a text from Jockey before. He was always the one to contact me. *Always!*

Beneath my annoyance with him for not getting in touch since his birthday, I was quietly confident I'd be getting a text from him very soon. It was Friday after all—bro-job night. But I was only going if he text me to come over. I wasn't giving the bastard the satisfaction of seeing me turn up uninvited. I didn't want to give him the impression I had enjoyed the other night.

Gavin flexed an ankle, his toes digging into my thigh.

"Hate your feet," I grumbled.

His eyes didn't leave the television. "No you don't."

Sighing, I tossed my head onto the sofa's back. "We really need to get a bigger couch."

"Or you could just go sit on the armchair."

"But it's easier to watch the game from here."

"You've never been a rugby fan before so I don't imagine you'll mind moving to the cheap seats if my feet bother you that much."

His feet weren't really the problem, but I couldn't tell him that.

I didn't respond, and when his look finally drifted my way, it teased a path down the side of my neck. "Nice sweater," he said with a piss-taking grin.

"Cut it out."

"So when are you going to introduce me to the sexy vampire of yours?"

My sexy vampire was the name he'd come up with for the mystery woman he assumed had covered me in root rash. Little did he know the mystery woman was a slender six-foot labourer with a pair of big hairy balls.

"Never," I said. "I haven't seen her again."

"That's a shame. I would have liked to meet her."

"Why? So you could make fun of me?"

"No. So I can make sure you're sowing your wild oats in the right sort of places."

"I'd rather you keep your nose out of my wild oats if you don't mind."

Gavin let out a throaty chuckle. "Speaking of sowing wild oats... do you mind if I go out for dinner with Fiona this evening?"

"Why would I mind?"

"Well... you've just been a little clingy lately. So I thought you might rather I stay home if there's something bothering you. Fiona won't mind coming here."

"I haven't been clingy. And there's nothing bothering me."

"My spidey senses tell me otherwise."

"Your spidey senses are malfunctioning."

He looked at me with a frown, expression a little concerned. "Well, you know I'm here if you need to talk."

"I'm fine. And I'm just missing Brian. That's all."

"Has he still not called?"

"Not yet. But I'm sure he's just busy settling in to his new schedule." I don't know who I was trying to kid. Me or Gavin.

"The best thing you could do is forget all about him," Gavin said bluntly. "Brian's a dick."

"He's my best mate."

"A lot of school friendships come to an end when high school finishes. Even the ones with best mates."

"You and Trent are still best mates."

"But that's different."

"How?"

"Because Trent and I were both working class boys. Same upbringing. Same morals. Same expectations. Rich folk aren't like us. It's just the way it is. Sure, I'll admit Brian is a nice enough boy but something like this was always bound to happen. To be honest, I'm surprised you two stayed mates as long as you did considering you're from different sides of the tracks." He quickly added, "And just so you know, we're from the better side."

"Really? Because this mansion of ours is about as big as his parent's lounge."

"Money ain't everything, matey."

"Says the man who prays he wins lotto every week."

"Don't get me wrong, I'd love to be loaded. But I wouldn't want to grow up with money the way Brian has. He'll never know what it's like to be on this side of the fence. To take pleasure from the small things like you and I do."

Gavin's philosophy was the stuff of working-class fairy tales. The ones where we're told by Hollywood that the poor are kinder and more generous, and wealthier in the ways that matter the most. It was all bullshit. If that were the case there wouldn't be so many violent muggings in poor neighbourhoods or teens huffing glue down the alleyways behind shops.

"Life is a bit like one of your video games," Gavin said as he sat there like some blue-collar guru. "But the thing is we don't all start off playing the game at the same level. A lad like Brian is playing the beginner's level. Easy street. It's all safe and happy and fluffy bunnies. He's bound to win and clock the game. It's set up that way. But it's also boring as hell because the ending is already programmed. It's predictable. But our side of the fence is much more exciting..." He waggled his eyebrows like he was telling a dirty joke. "We start the game at a much harder level. We ain't shooting no fluffy bunnies, we're bazookering the shit out of zombie dogs and cannibal children. It's exciting because we never know what's gonna happen one day to the next. It might seem boring and repetitive, but it isn't really. And the exciting part is we don't know if we will clock the game. Not many of us do, but knowing that a few of us can is what makes it so much fun. And you've got the best chance of clocking the game at this level out of anyone I know."

"What makes you think that?"

He tapped the side of his head. "Spidey senses."

I smiled, realising this was part of the reason Gavin's company made me feel better. He only ever saw my potential, even if it were a figment of his imagination. "Thanks, Gavin."

We resumed watching the rugby match, although my gaze was aimed more at my phone than the television. It was now past seven o'clock and there was still no invite from Jockey.

He'll text soon, I assured myself. *He always does on a Friday.*

The horny fucker wouldn't want to miss out on sucking me off. He'd made it pretty clear the other night in the car how much he enjoyed my dick—and my feet apparently. If he were lucky I'd consider taking all my clothes off and laying down on his bed so he could get his jollies from seeing me fully naked. Maybe even let him rim my ass again.

Anal was out of the question though. He could suck me and rim me. And maybe kiss my feet again. But nothing else. It was important we revert back to normal and assume the positions we usually held. He was the cocksucker and I was the dude who got sucked. That's how it had been for nearly two years and it worked well. It suited us. Suited our friendship.

I suppose I could also suck his dick. Just for a little while. But then he will suck me for way longer. And swallow! Yep. He's definitely gotta swallow every load from now on.

The sofa rocked as Gavin shifted onto his back and spread his legs, now bent at the knees. "Do you fancy giving me a hand with Betsy this weekend? Trent reckons he's found me an old motor we can install in her."

"I don't know the first thing about installing a motor." My eyes drifted in the direction of the backyard where Betsy had been parked motionless for eight years. "I'd be more of a hindrance than a help."

"I don't know what I'm doing either. We can learn together."

"How can we learn together if we don't have a clue what we're doing?"

"Trent said we can follow a tutorial on YouTube. He said it should be a piece of piss."

"I can see that going well. Not."

"Nar, she'll be right."

"Famous last words."

"It's been ages since you've helped me work on the old girl. It'll be fun."

"That's because I'm not twelve anymore and I know we're never driving to the south island in the death trap."

"Oi, that death trap has a name," he joked, resting his feet across my lap. "And feelings."

I was completely unbothered by the presence of Gavin's feet on my lap until he reached down and scratched his nuts, the innocent adjustment leaving the nylon pants he wore clinging to his bulge so that it clearly outlined the contours of his dick and balls.

Images of Jockey spearing my asshole invaded my brain and I shoved his feet off my lap. "Keep your trotters to yourself."

"You're cruel you are." He swung his feet to the floor and leaned back into the cushions. "And here I was thinking you might give me a foot rub."

"It'll be a cold day in hell before I touch those ugly things."

"My feet aren't ugly," he said, sounding genuinely offended. "Fiona reckons I've got sexy feet."

To be fair to Gavin his feet weren't ugly. Foot lovers like Jockey may have even thought they looked nice with their strong square toes, neatly trimmed nails, and soft dark hair dusting the tops. But that didn't mean I wanted to touch them.

Still staring down at his feet, Gavin added, "Fiona reckons they're one of my best features. Almost as good as my—"

"Cock," I said, seeing the punchline a mile away.

"I was going to say my personality."

"No you weren't."

He smirked. "Nar, I wasn't."

Once the game finished, Gavin went to go shower and get ready for his date with Fiona. Then he was out the door and gone, leaving me alone on the couch. The sun had now disappeared behind the western hills, out of sight, and the last rays of the day illuminated the thin, wispy clouds from below, so that they shone like pure gold.

There was still no text from Jockey, but I was too tired to get upset about it. *I'll just close my eyes for a moment*, I thought, leaning back into the sofa and propping my feet on the coffee table.

Sleep took me almost instantly.

THE FIRST RAP ON THE front door failed to wake me fully. I nuzzled my face into the soft fabric of the couch and scratched the side of my nose. *Gavin will get that*, I thought, my mind drifting between sleep and consciousness. The second knock was distinctly louder and brought me to my senses with a jolt.

Gavin's gone out, I suddenly remembered. I sat up and rubbed my eyes. Squinting at my phone, the time slowly came into focus. It was half past nine; I had been asleep for over an hour.

With a sigh, I got to my feet, stretched, and glanced out the window to see who it was.

Standing there with a six-pack of beer was Jockey. To my surprise, his spontaneous arrival gave me an unexpected thrill in the pit of my stomach. Forcing away the smile that threatened to breach my lips, I went to let him in. I stood to one side, allowing him past, then closed the door.

Walking past me into the kitchen, he said, "You didn't turn up so I thought I could come here for a change."

When he turned around to face me, I gave him a quick head-to-toe glance taking in what he had on. The green camo pants and red shirt were just tight enough to reveal his thighs' lithe lines, the wiry muscles of his arms. The shirt was unbuttoned one button past modest, giving me a glimpse of his tanned chest. I finally gave myself permission to smile. I had won the battle of patience.

It looked like I'd be getting my cock sucked tonight after all.

Chapter 3

JOCKEY AND I FOUND ourselves jeering and shouting at the two figures circling each other viciously on the flat screen. What had started as a short, friendly battle of tactile memory and dexterous thumbs on the couch had rapidly spiralled into a two-hour, all-out war on the floor, as close to the scene of action as possible.

We would have normally got around to the real action by now but I think the fact we were at my house, and not getting stoned in his manky sleepout, may have skewered the normal routine a bit. But that was okay. I wasn't in a rush. There was a thrill in the building anticipation, knowing that at any moment he'd ask me to shut the Xbox down and suggest we watch some porn on his phone. The only thing I was disappointed by was he'd yet to make a comment about how I'd paused the game an hour ago to remove my shoes and socks to reveal my bare feet he'd told me he loved so much. But the night was still young, I reminded myself.

I furiously tapped on my controller, my reflexes punching in combinations faster than he could think them up.

"You've got to be kidding me, what the hell!" My brow furrowed in tense concentration. I slashed downwards with my sword, spinning around to avoid Jockey's spinning drop kick.

"Fucking hell!" I swore as my character sustained serious damage from a surprise-backhand body-spike combo. Grimly eyeing my rapidly deteriorating life bar, I looked away in disgust as my character was thrown to the ground with a dirty combination.

"Does anyone know how much of an asshole your gaming alter-ego is?" I muttered darkly. I slid a glare to the teeth baring, hunched over gargoyle that had morphed from my usually happy-go-lucky friend. It had always been like this— regardless of who you were to him, when Jockey had a console in his hands, nothing mattered except his opponent's total annihilation.

His gleeful whoop and victorious howl had me quickly turning back to the screen to see my character lying broken and defeated in a heap on the arena floor.

I threw back my head in frustration. "How are you beating me?!" I groaned. The glimpse of Jockey's satisfied smirk from the corner of my eye had me snapping back up as I turned to glare at him.

Something in Jockey's smug snicker had suspicion flashing through me. "You asshole. There's no way... You're cheating, aren't you?" The answering quirk of Jockey's lips all but confirmed it. "Bastard!" I tossed aside my controller and narrowed my eyes menacingly at the cheating fucker.

"Now, now," Jockey soothed, holding out his hands placatingly. His amused, entertained laughter as he tried to roll away from my playful punch calmed me down. Rubbing his shoulder for dramatic effect, he said, "I think it might be time for us to play a different game."

"What game would that be?"

"One where I can take care of this." His gaze pointed down to the crotch of his pants. There was a firm mound there. "I've been nursing a boner since you took your shoes and socks off."

"So you did notice!"

"How could I not?" He reached over and ran his palm up and down my calf muscle. "I told you how sexy your feet are."

I gazed down at my bare feet with approval, admiring their sleek shape and high arches. "They are pretty nice, aren't they?"

Jockey laughed. "Sounds like someone's getting himself a big ego."

"How can I not when someone's dick gets so big from looking at me?" I cringed inwardly, worried if that flirty comeback crossed the line.

Jockey rolled with it though and returned with, "Maybe it's best you take a look to see how big it is." Lying back, he raised his butt off the floor and shucked his jeans and cotton boxers down till they bunched at his dusty work boots. He slowly rose back to a sitting position, like he was doing one long, sexy sit-up. His cock stretched towards me as he scratched his balls with one hand. I swallowed.

I should have been asking him why his dick was being unleashed when it was my cock that was about to get sucked. But my ability to speak momentarily vanished as I stared in awe at his sizable meat.

Gaze fixed on mine; his lips were slightly parted as if dirty words were about to leap forward from his tongue. He was oozing heat, and confidence, and maleness. His gaze briefly flicked from my eyes to his cock and back again. "You okay?" he asked.

"Sorry...I just." I coughed softly. "I can't believe that's been inside me."

"Yeah, bro. You did good." He wrapped his finger around the shaft, squeezing until a pearly bead of precum slipped out the slit. "That's a lot of cock for a virgin but you took it like a natural."

I didn't like the way he worded that, but I nodded anyway. After all, the statement wasn't incorrect. It was a lot of cock for a virgin to take.

Still mesmerized by the sight of his beautiful prick, I got a shock when Jockey leaned down and grabbed my feet and swung them onto his lap. He paused, examining my bare feet with his tickling fingertips, tracing the instep and sole of each before digging deeper to run along the paths made by the bones.

I groaned in approval when his thumbs pressed into the soft flesh under the arch of my foot.

"Were you sore the next day?" he whispered. "After I fucked you?"

"A little bit."

He raised my left foot to his face and blew against the underside of my toes. "Did it feel weird having my come inside you?"

"I guess so."

"That's why I could never let a guy bugger me. I'd hate knowing his baby batter was up there painting the inside of my ass." He glanced at me briefly and a contemptuous smile played on his lips for a moment. "And the thought of shitting him out afterwards. No thanks."

I was too zoned out from what he was doing to my feet to pay much attention to what he was saying. I could just imagine Gavin's reaction if he walked in right now and found me getting my feet rubbed while Jockey sat there with a raging hard-on.

"I liked how you called out my name while I was fucking you." He let out a shuddering breath as he rubbed my foot against his cock. "That made me feel good."

"Did it?"

"Mmm. Made me feel like the man. No one's ever called my name out like you did." His gaze turned cold, almost predatory. "It was as if my cock belonged up your ass."

"Well, I'm glad you enjoyed your present."

"I'm not the only one who enjoyed it. You came too."

"Yeah."

"You came so fucking hard, bro. And you weren't even touching your cock!" He snicker-snorted. "My big dick fucked the come right out of your balls. That was so epic."

"Would you like a medal or something?" Now I was getting pissed off.

"No medal needed. Just being able to rub these sexy feet of yours is all the reward I need." A long lick from heel to toes followed the compliment. "I'm starting to think you might be giving me a foot fetish."

"I bet you say that to all the girls," I joked.

"Only the ones who let me fuck them raw."

He must have seen the flash of anger in my eyes because he very fucking quickly started showering my feet with kisses, subduing my annoyance, which I imagine was his plan. He must have known that if he threw my needy ass enough compliments then he could push us into more awkward territory.

"How long did you keep my load inside you for?"

"Does it matter?"

"I'm just curious."

"Until the next morning, if you must know."

"So you went to bed with me still inside you?" His eyes widened like he couldn't quite believe it. "Slept with my cum inside you all night?"

I nodded, reminding myself to remain calm.

"Did you leak much on the way home?" he asked.

"What?" I'd heard him perfectly fine, but couldn't believe he was asking me this.

Jockey gave my foot a quick lick before repeating the question, "Did you leak into your undies after I fucked you? I only ask cos it felt like I gave you a huge load and so I just wondered if you had any leakage."

"I'm not a milk bottle."

"You were a milk bottle that night." Another lick. "You were filled with Jockey milk."

I felt my cheeks roasting with a blush. The asshole was enjoying this. But the problem was I was also enjoying this foot rub and didn't want it to stop prematurely by snapping at him.

"So was there leakage?" he asked again.

"Yes, Jockey," I said exasperatedly. "Some of your sperm leaked out of my ass and into my undies. Enough to leave stains and get my balls wet." I had hoped a blunt and detailed response would cure him of his nosiness. It didn't.

"Have you washed them yet?"

"Why the hell do you wanna know that?"

"Why do you think?" He grinned, unabashed. "I wanna see the stains."

I could tell this was turning him on by the amount of precum leaking out his cock right now. *Fucking freak.*

Another dark smile played across his face. "You haven't washed them, have you? Go get them so I can see."

"I'm not showing you my cummy undies, bro. That's just wrong."

"Go on. It's my cum."

"Dude you're really starting to piss me ooooffff." My voice broke like a pubescent boy as Jockey sucked my big toe into his mouth. "Oh my God. That feels good. So good."

He chuckled around my toe then moved down the row, sucking each one like it was a tiny cock. Then he moved onto my other foot, giving each of those piggies the same treatment. When he was finished deepthroating my toes, he put on his sweetest voice and asked, "Can I see the undies...please?"

With a resentful sigh, I nodded. "Fine."

"You're the best." He let go of my foot so I could get up.

I went to my room and hunted for the cum-stained briefs in the dirty pile of laundry behind my door. I probably should have told him to get fucked and not be such a weirdo, but I also felt strangely flattered by how keen he was to see them. When I returned to the lounge, Jockey was still sat on the floor but with one noticeable difference—all his clothes were off and tangled in a messy pile atop of his work boots. He sat with his long, hairy legs spread wide, his cock flying high and hard from its nest of dark-brown pubes.

I pretended like his nudity was normal and avoided looking at that cherry-popping cock of his. "Here," I said, handing him the soiled briefs. "Had I known you were gonna be such a perve about this I would have washed these days ago."

Jockey wasted no time turning them inside-out, inspecting the dried cum still stuck to the material. "I knew I'd given you heaps," he said, smiling with pride. "Look at it all!"

Oh how I wish I could say he was exaggerating, but he wasn't. The stains were worse than I remembered. Mind you, I hadn't exactly inspected them after taking them off. I'd just buried them under my washing pile in the hopes of forgetting.

"Did you jerk off with them?" he asked excitedly.

"Why the hell would I wanna jerk off with them?"

"To remember your first time."

"Considering you left me with a thousand lovebites which have been on my neck all week, all I've needed to do to remember my first time is to look in the mirror."

He snorted. "Sorry about that, bro. I think I got a bit carried away."

"Ya think?"

I finally sat back down beside him and waited for him to resume the foot rub but he was too fascinated by my undies to even glance in the direction of my feet. While he studied the cum-stained briefs, my gaze lingered over that hard dick of his that really did put mine to shame. My jealousy was minimal though to the desire throbbing in my own cock, and I very nearly reached over to touch his prick and squeeze his girth. Thankfully I had enough pride not to do that.

"Would it be okay if I keep these? You know...as a souvenir of my birthday?

"Sure. They're all yours." I was past trying to understand what made this man's filthy mind tick.

"I can give you twenty bucks for them if you want?"

"It's fine, Jockey. You keep them."

"Thanks, Mikey," he said, then smothered the undies over his mouth and nose, inhaling the stains.

"You're grim, mate."

He turned to me; face still covered with the briefs as he took a second hit. "That's definitely my boys in there," he said. "I know my own smell."

"You do know you're also smelling my ass sweat?"

"I know. I reckon the scents go well together, don't you?" He held the undies towards me for a sniff.

"Hell no. I am not sniffing those."

"Don't you wanna know what we smell like?"

"*We*?"

"Yeah. That's both of us in there, bro." When I refused to sniff them he returned them to his own nose and inhaled again. "I always thought you and me made a good team. This smell proves it."

"Why don't you smell the front while you're at it," I muttered sarcastically.

And guess what? He did. Of course he fucking did.

"I was joking, dork."

"I know," he replied through the mask of my underwear. "But I was gonna smell the front when I got home anyway."

"How many fucking times did your mother drop you on the head when you were a baby?"

"Twice apparently." He took another deep sniff of the front then lowered my undies to his lap. "But that doesn't change the fact your dick sweat smells just as good as my cum and your ass."

"Good to know."

He bunched my undies into a tight ball and then leaned over to put them away in the pocket of his discarded pants. He then leaned back, smiling expectantly as he scratched his balls.

"What?" I asked.

"It ain't gonna suck itself." His gaze pointed down at his dick. "Come on."

I was taken aback by his arrogance, but not surprised. I'd been well aware that our Friday night fun would probably become more of a two-way street after what had happened on his birthday. Provided he didn't expect to fuck me again, and sucked me off for twice as long, then I was okay with sucking him off.

Slowly, I leaned down toward Jockey's dick. Halfway there, his hand came down on my neck, forcing me the rest of the way. I felt the thick, warm head of his cock against my mouth and opened to it. Jockey groaned.

"That's it," he said.

I took as much as I could into my mouth. Jockey's hand was insistent, pushing me farther down until I started to choke. Still Jockey pushed. I resisted, but his touch was firm, and finally I had to just relax and let Jockey fill my mouth. I felt the rough hair of Jockey's belly against my nose, smelled sweat and manliness.

"I bet you've been thinking about my cock ever since I fucked you," he said.

Unable to respond, I moved my mouth up and down Jockey's shaft. His hand never left my neck, working like a piston to control my movements. My throat began to burn as it was scraped by the thick head. Jockey continued to talk, his voice droning in my ears.

"Suck that big prick," he said. "Suck it nice and slow."

I told myself to stay cool, and to remember that it was my turn next and I could pay him back with the dirty talk.

"Oh, yeah," Jockey growled. "Milk my fucking balls, faggot."

I recoiled at the word. Had Jockey just called me a fag? Pushing against his grip, I raised my head. "What did you say?"

"Suck my cock," Jockey replied, trying to push me back down.

I pulled away. "I'm not a fag."

Jockey looked at me and laughed. "Tell that to my dick," he said, reaching out and grabbing my t-shirt, pulling me toward him.

Our gazes locked, faces only inches apart. I couldn't tell if he was about to bite me or kiss me. He did neither and whispered, "Suck it, bitch."

My head was pushed back down to his lap, my mouth forced around his invading cock. My tongue ran over it on its way past, deep into me. I gagged and tried to pull away, but his hand prevented it. I could have struggled free but something made me obey the hand keeping me down there.

"Ah, shit, yeah, suck it, man." He ran his fingers through my hair as I slathered my tongue over the helmeted ridge of his glans. His tight little piss slit oozed a droplet of liquid—much sweeter than I had expected.

With my face firmly rooted to his cock, Jockey lay on his back and started thrusting his hips up into my face, fucking my throat. His deep grunts and choppy breaths were like a drug to me, and I felt my own cock throb as his pleasure grew and grew. With one hand, he used his fingertip to trace my lips around him, and the other hand remained threaded in my long hair, guiding me, controlling the rhythm of our union.

The smell of his damp crotch continued to assault my senses, letting me know he hadn't showered since finishing work. I should have been revolted but I found myself appreciating the sour-spicy flavour of a man who'd busted his ass working manual labour, his blue-collar ball sweat triggering something primal in me.

While my mouth serviced Jockey's tool, my hands went on a mission of their own, exploring the hard terrain of his sinewy body—hairy calves to bony shoulders. Every inch of the way I clutched and grabbed his toned flesh, eager to learn the feel of Jockey Savage's body. I left his cock to nuzzle his balls, and used my mouth to taste him. I licked the smooth skin of his inner thighs, explored those tight abs, washed the fuzzy trail of hair below his navel with my tongue, eventually making my way up to his hair-glazed pecs where I stopped to suck and nibble one of his tiny, hard nipples. I was about to go higher and kiss him, wrap his tongue with mine, but his strong hands pushed the top of my head, demanding my mouth return to his cock.

"You like stoner cock?" he asked while I pawed his hairy thighs, shoving his crotch closer to my face. I choked as his dick hit my tonsils. As I pulled it out, a thick sting of drool trailed from the head of his cock to my lips.

"Yeah, I like stoner cock." I lapped his boner again. "But I think it might be time for the stoner to suck my cock."

Silence. Silence. Silence.

"I can't do that I'm afraid," Jockey finally answered.

"Don't be a tease. I've been hanging out for a blowie all week, man." I shuffled away and unzipped my jeans, wrestled my hard dick out so it was ready for him. When he didn't move, I said to him, "Come on. It's my turn."

"Put your cock away, Mike. I'm not sucking it."

"And why the fuck not?"

"I'm not being rude but I can't suck the dick of a lesser male."

"A lesser male?" I half-shrieked.

"I still respect you as a mate and as a person... just not sexually or as a man so much."

Tension built in my shoulders so sharply that an ache worked its way up to my neck. "Where the hell has this come from?"

He looked at me like I was an idiot. "Do I really have to spell it out for you?"

"It looks a lot fucking like it, Jockey."

"I came inside you, bro. You gave up the goods. Took it like a bitch. Took it like a bitch on—"

"Okay. Okay. I get the fucking point!"

"It's a bit like being in the army. You used to outrank me so I'd happily take orders from you but now you're just a private and I'm the captain."

Typical Jockey, finding a way to bring it back to some sort of army bullshit.

"Don't get me wrong, I really enjoyed fucking your pussy and I'd be keen to give it a feed again but it would have to be on my terms."

"I don't have a pussy, you dick."

A callous laugh bubbled out of him. "You watch porn so you know as well as I do that any hole that takes a cock is called a pussy."

In the crudest terms he did have a point, but I still didn't like being told I had a pussy. What had started as a fun night of mates hanging out had now turned into something toxic. We sat there in silence as I looked around the room deciding what object would be the most satisfying to hit him over the head with.

Jockey broke the silence with, "I'm sorry if I've upset you, bro, but I thought you'd just know things would change after I cornholed you."

"What the fuck is your problem?"

"I don't have one. I'm actually trying to be nice. That's why I didn't come here expecting a fuck."

"How is insulting me and not asking for a fuck, which you were never going to get by the way, being nice?"

"So you don't take on a role you're not cut out for."

"What are you talking about?"

"I'm talking about you being my faggot."

It was another verbal slap. But I could tell by the way he said that word he didn't mean it as a casual insult. But I could tell it wasn't meant as a compliment either.

"If you agreed to be my faggot then sure... I'd suck your dick now and then. Ain't nothing wrong with that. You know I like your cock. But I'm not sucking a faggot's dick who doesn't belong to me."

"You're not making any sense."

"Me blowing you before was always me being a mate. But me fucking you changed that. As an alpha male I won't suck a lesser man's cock unless I own him."

"Own him!?"

"Yeah. If you're my faggot then that makes you my property."

"What Andrew Tate bullshit is this?"

"It's just the way the world works, dog. It's human nature, y'know what I mean? There are leaders and there are followers. Alphas and betas. Real men and faggots." He took his life in his hands with what he added next, "And I think you know now which one you are."

It's official. You're insane. Just like everyone in town says you are.

I had been given a front row seat into Jockey's view on sex, and it was every bit as depraved and nutty as I'd always imagined. But just because it was loopy didn't make me feel any less insulted.

"I know you're angry with me, I get that, but if it's any consolation the fact I'd even consider taking you on as my faggot is a huge compliment. There's not many guys I'd do that for."

"How exactly is that a compliment?"

"Because a guy would have to be hot as fuck for me to wanna fuck him every day."

The meaning behind his words tore through me in a hot wave of confusion. "You... you want to fuck me every day?"

"The more important question is do you want me to fuck you every day?"

I hesitated. Why the fuck did I hesitate. "No," I finally said. "I want you to suck my cock."

"And I've told you that's not happening." His hooded gaze lingered on my crotch. "Now are you gonna finish the blowjob or are you going to keep being difficult?"

"What do you think, dipshit?"

Instead of responding to my pissy comment, he laid flat on his back and started to masturbate.

"What the fuck, Jockey?" The sentence was more of a choked out cry, but Jockey didn't seem to notice, seeing as he was fully engrossed in tossing off. I wanted to keep arguing but the randomness of his action soon had me spellbound. Sat there with a dumb look on my face, I took in the full sight of my friend sprawled naked on the floor, finishing what I had started. Despite his skinny physique, he was still well-proportioned—toned from hard work but lean from genetics. His skin looked soft and luminescent; a tasty treat for any tongue that dared to lick flat the hairs on his chest. And that's what I would have done if I wasn't so angry with him right now.

In less than a minute, he was grunting as his cock ejaculated all over his tanned stomach and chest, a few errant drops glistening on the carpet. When his breathing returned to normal, he sat up and grabbed his underwear to wipe his front clean.

"Why'd you do that? I would have kept sucking you. All you had to do was agree to suck me off too."

He didn't speak. Just stood up and began to put his clothes on. I felt a surge of panic.

"What are you doing?" I demanded. "You're not leaving, are you?"

"I think it's best I go. We're only gonna end up arguing if I stay."

"We're only gonna argue because you're being fucking mental and unreasonable."

Jockey sat, half-dressed on the edge of the couch, in just his t-shirt and a single sock, its companion hanging limply in his left hand. He regarded me with the kind of blank expression that was infuriating.

"Don't look at me like that," I snapped. "You are being unreasonable."

"If you say so, Mike," he said in a wooden voice. He put on the other sock and reached for his pants.

"Can you at least give me a handy real quick?" My desperation escalated as I watched him put his pants on and slipped on his boots. "Please, Jockey? Just a few tugs. I'm horny as fuck. I've been like it ever since you fucked me."

He smiled and I thought I was about to get some relief but all he said was, "Thanks for the undies. Give me a call when you've calmed down." He raised his hand in a little wave and turned on his heel.

I watched him go before looking down and seeing he'd left his cum-streaked boxers behind. Fuelled by rage, I picked them up and went and put them in the bin. The same place our friendship now was.

Chapter 4

"I love rock n roll so put another dime in the juke box, babeeee."

Gavin's dreadful singing floated down the hall, noisily making its way into my bedroom and unwilling eardrums. I rolled onto my side and pulled the pillow over my head with a groan. It wasn't so much that his voice was terrible, which it most definitely was, it was how fucking happy he sounded.

He had been meeting up with Fiona every night after work, either taking her out for Fish and Chips or inviting her back here for a drink, which usually then led to the pair going to bed early and doing what it was that was making Gavin so happy lately. I don't think the inside of our fridge had seen a wine bottle since my mother ran off, but the huckery old whiteware was now permanently stocked with Passion Pop, the wine of choice for underage girls and men like Gavin who couldn't afford to spend too much on impressing a woman.

I should have got up already but for the past hour, I had been staring at the bedroom ceiling. In the far corner, a tiny black spider was industriously repairing its web. Mesmerised, I watched as it plucked at the silk thread, oblivious to the world and my foul mood below. God, how I envied the spider.

I reached across the bed and pulled back the curtain a couple of centimetres. The sun had already cleared the ridge of hills opposite and was now inching its way across a cloudless blue sky. It hadn't rained anywhere in the North Island for weeks, and by the looks of it, today wasn't going to be any different. The six o'clock news the previous evening had led with the story of a Waikato farmer whose business was on the brink of collapse.

"How do you feel?" the grinning news anchor had asked, the camera panning across what had once been a lush green paddock but now looked more like barren wasteland.

"Fucking marvellous," I had replied on the farmer's behalf and had changed the channel without watching any more.

I gazed out the window. The trees in Mrs Avery's yard were in full bloom. The elderly widow was the only one on the block who had a nice garden. I watched as a tui flitted happily from tree to tree, the white tuft on its throat gleaming in the morning sunshine. Between nature showing off how pretty it was on a summer's day and Gavin's joyous wailing down the hall, my foul mood felt very out of place.

It had been four days since Jockey had come to visit and I still hadn't recovered. I was so fucking embarrassed. But mostly I was pissed off. How could I not be angry with him? Jockey, the most uncool prick in town, had rejected me. Fuck, if there was one person I was higher up the social ladder than then it was undoubtedly that numbnuts.

He'd always seemed so grateful to suck my cock, made it seem like it was the highlight of his week, and now he was saying 'no thanks' and expecting me to service him instead. Like what the fuck?

If Jockey thought I was going to play by his rules then he was sadly mistaken. There was no way I was going to give the overgrown fuck-knuckle what he wanted. Unlike Jockey I actually had some pride. I wasn't going to spend my Friday nights letting some dude treat my face like a cum sock.

According to the wannabe soldier I had three choices: we could be mates with no sex at all (which was probably the sensible option), or we could continue an oral only agreement where I remained the sole cocksucker (Hell-to-the-no), or I could agree to a deal where he could fuck me as much as he liked in exchange for the occasional blowjob (Never-gonna-fucking-happen-dot-com).

At this stage I was tempted for a fourth option: not be friends at all. But the sad reality was I wasn't exactly flushed with mates myself. Not now with Brian gone. Socially-speaking, I needed Jockey just as much as he needed me.

Does he need me though?

Jockey hadn't reached out since he'd left my house, ditching those stanky boxers of his in his mad rush, and I was beginning to think maybe he was more okay with his own company than I was.

Speaking of those stanky boxers, they'd only stayed in the bin ten minutes before I went and rescued them. That's when I had done the unthinkable; taken them to my room and jerked off while I licked the residue of his cum. And once I'd licked that all up, I smelled them. Front and back. Familiarising myself with his smells. After I'd ejaculated, covering my tummy in a pond of shame, I had promised myself it would never happen again and that the rancid garment was destined, once again, for the bin and that this time it would stay there.

They never made it to the bin a second time. I'd kept them in the top drawer beside my bed and had been smelling them every day. Several times a day. Anytime I needed a wank, which felt like all the time, I'd go shut myself in my room and slip Jockey's boxers over my head, breathing in his scent while I beat my dick.

And I think that is where most of my foul mood stemmed from. My anger wasn't just because he had rejected me, I was angry because I wanted him. Wanted him bad. Something about his smell down there, that male scent of sex, piss and musk, had me fantasising about doing things with Jockey I hadn't ever thought I would do. Yes, I wanted to suck his dick. Maybe even try swallowing his come. It was an embarrassing thing to admit but yeah...I was curious to taste him. More shameful was I think I'd let him fuck me again too. I had tried telling myself that night at the beach was enjoyable because I was drunk. But I knew now it wasn't that. I had liked it because I liked the way he moved his dick. Liked the way his long, lean body felt above me. Liked how I'd never been as connected to another person as I had with him in that sweaty, defiling moment.

But he can't have it all his own way!

Rolling over again, I glanced at the top drawer where I stored Jockey's boxers. As I reached down to rub my cock, I weighed up if I should have a quick wank with them. Of course I should. No better way to start the day than emptying one's balls.

I pulled the blanket back, exposing my naked body, then reached over to open the drawer.

Two quiet knocks sounded on my door.

I quickly covered myself up. "Yeah?"

The door opened and Gavin walked in. "Hey, sleepy head. Don't you have work this morning?"

I shook my head. "Not until eleven."

"Oh. My bad. I guess I'll leave you to sleep some more."

"It's okay. That beautiful singing voice of yours woke me up already."

"Sorry." He smiled apologetically. "I didn't realise I was singing so loud."

"That's cool. I'm gonna get up now anyway."

"Good. Because Fiona went out and bought us bagels for breakfast." He smiled like a kid at Christmas. "Isn't she the best?"

I nodded while keeping my true answer to myself.

Gavin closed the door again and I rolled out of bed, scrunching my toes on the carpet. My gaze looked longingly at the top drawer then down at my semi-erect cock, It looked like my wank would have to wait.

When I walked into the kitchen I saw Gavin sat at the table while Fiona stood near the sink plating up the bagels she had brought over. Gavin looked like a little kid waiting for his mum to serve up yummy pancakes. His white-socked toes curled around the bottom rung of the chair, his hands clasped together.

As soon as Fiona placed the plate down on the table, Gavin and I reached out like feral street children to get one each.

"How have you been, Mike?" Fiona asked me.

My mouth was full and a bit of bagel fell on my lap as I replied with, "Good."

"Matthew told me you two had a lot of fun on his birthday."

I swallowed down the masticated bagel. "It was alright, I guess."

"Who's Matthew?" Gavin asked.

"Jockey," I replied as Fiona and I shared a look of frustration. We must have told Gavin this at least five times in the past fortnight but he still never managed to remember Jockey's real name.

"Matthew also told me you gave him his best birthday present ever," Fiona said. "That's high praise considering his aunt and uncle bought him that old ute for his eighteenth."

"What did you get him that was so good?" Gavin asked, his voice laced with suspicion. "My birthday's next month so I expect something just as good."

"Yes, what did you get him?" Fiona's expression turned sly. "Matthew wouldn't actually say. Just that it was the best present he's ever had."

Both set their eyes on me, waiting for a response.

I stilled, my heart beating weirdly hard, and just tried to keep my voice normal when I said, "A tinny from Max Mackey."

"That explains it." Gavin grinned knowingly. "That man's weed is legendary."

"I've heard that too," Fiona said. "My friend Dina keeps trying to buy from him but he insists he doesn't sell it anymore."

"He doesn't," Gavin said. "Unless you're the son of the woman he's still madly in love with."

Fiona looked confused. "Who are you talking about?"

Gavin pointed at me. "Max has been obsessed with Mike's mum for years. He probably thinks Mike might put in a good word for him with Joy."

"I can understand that," Fiona said thoughtfully. "I used to see Joy in the clubs back in the day. I always thought she was exceptionally beautiful. Which is why I'm sure Mike is such a handsome young man."

I wished that were true but I didn't look anything like Mum. And I certainly didn't consider myself that level of attractive.

"Sounds like I've got myself some competition." Gavin leaned over and ruffled my long hair, sending my long honey-blond fringe to fall in front of my eyes. "I always knew young Michael here would grow into a panty wetter. Live with a stud like me long enough and the good-looks just rub off."

"I think that might be a case of wishful thinking," Fiona teased him.

Smoothing my fringe back in place, I reached for another bagel. I'd promised myself to only have one to be polite but they tasted better than I'd expected.

"Will you be visiting Matthew today?" Fiona asked me. "If you see him tell him I'll be round this weekend."

"You like to spend a lot of time with this ex of yours." Gavin said it as a joke but it was obvious he was a bit iffy.

"I'm actually going there to visit his aunt. Jocelyn and I are friendly." Fiona then giggled playfully. "Besides, Matthew has his eye on someone else."

"Who?" Gavin and I asked in unison.

"Some cute little blond virgin apparently. I should probably say *they used to be a virgin* until according to Matthew he had this blond screaming out his name down at the beach."

He fucking told you!

Gavin sniggered. "As long as you're not the cute little blond calling out his name."

"I'm not," I snapped defensively.

Gavin gave me a strange look. "I was talking about Fiona, numbnuts. Chill out." Thankfully he didn't give my shameful outburst a second thought and returned his attention to his girlfriend. "You don't think Jockey is just telling you sexy stories to try and make you jealous?"

Fiona shook her head. "God no. Those days are long gone. Matthew's tastes these days are a little more...unique."

"Unique how?" Gavin asked.

"It's hard to explain. But he's certainly very taken by this blond of his. He didn't spare any detail; let me tell you." She fanned herself, feigning hotness. "Talk about steamy. That's why I had to come over and see you. It just put me in the mood to be near my man."

If the bagel didn't taste so delicious I would have barfed it up right then and there in protest at my ears falling victim to this bullshit.

"In that case..." Gavin's fingers slid up and down Fiona's arm. "Maybe you should tell me the story?"

Please don't.

"I don't think that would be appropriate," she said, eyes pointing at me. "It's pretty dirty."

"Pfft. Don't worry about, Mike. I'm sure he's heard me talk about worse. Besides, he's probably already heard the story from Jockey."

"I have," I said, "which is why I don't have to hear it again."

"Go in the lounge then," Gavin said bluntly. "I wanna hear the story."

Grabbing myself another bagel, I headed to the lounge and sat on the couch. I didn't turn on the television though. I wanted to hear this, just not be seen to want to.

It was silent for a while until I heard Fiona lower her voice to a sexy tone I'd never heard her use before. "Well...apparently Matthew tied this girl to a chair for two hours, hooked her up to some sort of sex toy that made her have multiple orgasms. He'd put a gag in her mouth so she couldn't scream, she had to sit there the whole time and take it while he sat and watched her squirm and come repeatedly."

Gavin laughed. "The kinky little fucker."

"After forcing her to orgasm multiple times he got down and started kissing her feet. Sucking her toes. Telling her how beautiful her feet were." Fiona's voice paused and I heard he take a sharp intake of breath. "Matthew said her feet were perfect. High arches, nicely-shaped toes. Said they even smelled sexy. Had him leaking all over the floor."

"Nothing wrong with complimenting a woman if she has beautiful feet," Gavin said greasily. "Like you do, baby."

I heard the sound of a quick smooch before Fiona continued with the story. "So...after he let her out of the kinky chair they went to the beach together and Matthew made her take all her clothes off. Inspected her body. Licked her out, front and back. Fingered her to get her ready for her first time...made sure that tight, virgin pussy was nice and wet and ready for his cock."

Fiona's voice was like an invisible hand stroking my balls, her words fire to my loins. I couldn't believe she was telling Gavin this story.

"And?" Gavin asked, his voice tight. "Keep going? This is a good story."

"And then he fucked her like a common slut."

"He what?" Gavin sounded stunned. "That's not on."

"But she wanted it, baby." Fiona said in a purr-like whisper. "She told him she was his bitch. Jockey's bitch. She was panting and moaning, so loud, so very, very loud. Matthew was worried people might hear her, that's how loud her moans were. She was so loud he had to put one of his socks in her mouth to shut her up."

That never happened!

"The dirty little slut just couldn't get enough of his big dick. Said it made her realise how beneath him she really was. She was just so pleased to be used by a real man who knew what he was doing. A man who knew how to hit that pussy just right."

Gavin's worried voice sounded next. "Jockey has a big dick?"

"In his version of the story he does," Fiona said with a giggle. "Doesn't every man think that of themselves?"

I half-expected Gavin to ask his girlfriend if Jockey was telling the truth about having a big dick but instead he said, "So what happened next?"

A few beats of silence, then, "Jockey! Jockey! Jockey! Ohhh Jockey. Fuck me harder Jockey. I'm yours!"

Fiona's impersonation of my orgasmic cries had me blushing. The embarrassment was so strong that I forced myself to block out the next part of the story, unable to relive the shame. I didn't actively listen until Fiona was almost finished with the story of the virgin blond losing their cherry.

"Then he came inside her," Fiona whispered excitedly, "flooding that slut's pussy with so much cum she was leaking for the rest of the night. Making sure she'd go home knowing just what a dirty little bitch she is."

"Mmm. That's hot," Gavin mumbled.

So much for his stance on safe sex, I thought. *The moment he thinks I'm out of earshot he makes it quite clear he too enjoys a raw rider.*

Fiona let out a deep satisfied sigh. "Apparently Matthew visited this girl a few days later and made her give him the knickers she'd been wearing that night so he could add them to his collection. Matthew says he's hung them above his bed so anyone who visits can see evidence of his latest conquest."

He better fucking not have!

There was another span of silence before Fiona's voice came back: "He said they are absolutely covered in come stains. The girl leaked into them all night and hadn't washed them for nearly a week. Just held onto them like she was proud of how had she'd been fucked like a whore."

"This blond sounds like a real dirty girl," Gavin said. "Just the way I like them."

Kissing noises followed.

"It *feels* like you enjoyed that story," I heard Fiona say.

Gavin laughed. "A little bit."

"I think you enjoyed it more than a little bit." Fiona let out an exaggerated gasp. "You've leaked precum all through your boxers, baby. We need to get you into clean ones."

The next thing I knew the horny lovebirds were walking past the lounge in the direction of Gavin's bedroom; the man's tented pants leading the way.

Chapter 5

ON MY WAY HOME FROM work that evening, I stopped off at the Chinese takeaways near my house to buy myself some dinner. I used the twenty dollars Gavin had given me this morning to pay for it. That was perhaps one of the few good things about the man spending every night with Fiona; he always left me money to buy myself dinner. I liked to think it was because he felt guilty but it probably had more to do with the fact he'd been too busy rooting to go buy us more groceries.

After ordering myself a tray of sweet and sour pork, I went next door to the dairy and bought myself a couple scratchie tickets. The only thing I usually won on them was a free ticket but I figured the short-lived thrill of pretending I might win something would be better than having a two dollar coin live in my wallet for weeks on end.

Tucking the two tickets in my wallet, I returned to the takeaways and sat down to wait for my meal. I tried to busy myself with the stack of magazines on the table, but I struggled to get lost in the articles about celebrities I couldn't give two shits about. Instead my mind kept wandering back to the events of the last week and how I'd made my asshole a two-way street.

Between Brian being a dick, and Jockey sticking his in me, I wondered if it was time I started expanding my social horizons. It was a great idea in theory but the trouble was my options weren't great. Because Brian and I had been a tight duo for so long—and occasionally a trio with Jockey—that the few associates I had acquired during my early high school years were more like strangers to me now. Part of the reason for that was my own fault for not keeping in touch, but many of them had also kept a safe distance from me knowing about my association with a Savage. I'd always told them Jockey was harmless, but they had never believed me, insisting he was a thief just like his criminal siblings. To the best of my knowledge the only thing Jockey had ever stolen was my virginity.

Twenty minutes later, I was back home with my steaming hot tray of sweet and sour pork. The battered meat pieces and pinky sauce looked and smelled delicious but I barely pecked at it, my appetite missing in action. I let it cool down and then put in the fridge.

As I sat down to watch some Netflix, I remembered the scratchie tickets. As I scratched away the panels, I entertained the thought of what I would spend my winnings on. It was such a Gavin thing to do, but it was sort of fun. I didn't imagine winning the major prize of twenty grand—*I'm not greedy*—instead I thought how I would spend the ten thousand dollar prize.

Okay so maybe I am a little greedy.

I decided I would pay to get one of my manuscripts professionally edited, help whip it into shape so it would grab the attention of an agent. Then I'd maybe buy a cheap runabout car. And with what I had left over I'd make a surprise trip up to

Auckland to visit Brian and shout us both a big night out on the town.

The thought of having a night out with my best friend made me smile. It also made me feel less resentful towards him for ignoring me. *Maybe he is just busy. It's his first time ever living away from home. And he probably has loads of assignments to work on.* Deep down I knew that was wishful thinking though. Dude was ghosting me. Prick.

Thanks to my little daydream, and subsequent return to being bitter, I didn't spot that my scratching finger had just revealed three little pictures of a kiwifruit. "Ha! I won something." My excitement wasn't that extreme, assuming it was probably just ten bucks but when I looked at the bottom of the ticket and saw what prize corresponded with the kiwifruit I had to blink twice to make sure I wasn't imagining things.

"Five hundred dollars!" I blinked some more and peered more closely to make sure I wasn't imagining things. "Fucking hell. It really is five hundred!"

Leaping to my feet, I did myself a happy dance around the lounge, whooping and yahooing. Sure, it wasn't life changing but it would be week changing. And that was good enough for me.

Just as I was about to grab the phone and call Gavin there was a loud knock at the door. I put the ticket back in my wallet and went to the front door.

It was Damian Takarangi. And his bulging backpack.

"Hey, Mikey, Mike" he said with a smile, the whole greeting feeling rehearsed. "How's it going?"

"Good." I eyed his backpack suspiciously and wondered if this was a visit or a request to move in.

"You told me the other day I could swing by if I ever needed a shower." His words were fractured with unusual pauses, like a drunkard in a pub, trying to make a point. He raised an arm and sniffed his armpit and laughed. "Well, I need one in a bad way."

After only a brief moment of hesitation, I stepped aside and said, "Sure. Come in."

We went and sat in the lounge where Damian dropped the backpack to the floor with a loud thunk. He sat on a chair, his legs spread wide. He wore high-top white sneakers that were unlaced and held the cuffs of his jeans. He put his hands between his legs. "Have you got something to drink, like a beer maybe?"

"Um. Maybe. Let me go check."

I wasn't sure how wise it was to be serving the neighbourhood addict alcohol, but he didn't seem too wired this evening. Inside the fridge I found two beers of Gavin's sat neglected on the bottom shelf. I grabbed them and carried them back to the living room. Damian was toeing off his sneakers. He looked up.

"They're new," he said, pointing to the sneakers. "I just got given them yesterday, and they're tearing my feet up. But I ain't gonna turn down free shit." He took a beer from me and touched his stomach, grimacing. "My tummy's growling. Still haven't eaten today."

Real subtle, I thought. I returned to the kitchen and warmed up my leftover dinner, trying to remember where I had left my wallet, and feeling bad for thinking such a thought. I came back into the living room with a plate of the microwaved Chinese food.

Damian was stripped down to his underwear.

I stopped dead.

His brown chest was mostly smooth and capped with wide, dark nipples the size of half dollars. His belly button protruded; a tight knot surrounded by black fur. His legs were still spread but covered now with hair instead of denim. I stared at Damian's red silk boxers and the koru tattoo snaking up one of his thighs.

"Is it hot in here?" I asked the near naked man in my lounge.

"I came to have a shower, remember?" he replied as if I were an idiot for questioning his state of undress. "But I'll eat first if you don't mind." He took the plate of food from me without so much as a *thanks cunt* and started scoffing my leftovers. He didn't speak until he was finished, although he looked up from time to time to stare at me and make me squirm.

Finally, Damian put the plate down, belching softly. "Excuse me," he said.

He stood then and walked around the room. "You've lived here for a while haven't you?"

"Ten years."

"It's a nice home," he said. "I mean, it's poxy like every other house on the street but you've got nice stuff."

"Thanks?"

Damian's gaze homed in on Gavin's pride and joy that hung on the wall above the television: a framed All Black jersey signed by the legendary rugby player Sir Colin Meads. It was the only real thing of value in the house and I wondered if Damian knew that.

Stop thinking he's here to steal shit, I told myself. *He's a family friend.*

Referring to Damian Takarangi as a family friend may have been a slight exaggeration but I'd certainly known the former bouncer most of my life, and despite his current predicament of nursing a drug habit that saw him in and out of homelessness I had to remember that beneath his troubles was a good man at heart.

He walked in front of the bay window, holding open the curtains. I looked at his boxer-clad ass, wondering if it would be as hairy as his legs. The tuft of hair above his crack suggested it might be. "I saw you the other day." I heard Damian say. "You went into the bushes at Hickford Park."

Caught off guard, I stammered, unable to voice a response. Damian turned around and faced me. "I always wondered if you swung that way," he said, nodding knowingly.

I blanked, looked at the beer bottle in my hand as if it had just materialized there. What are you supposed to say to your former babysitter uninvited and undressed in your living room when they call out your sexuality?

"I just stopped there to take a piss."

He smirked. "That's what they all say."

I wasn't about to let this addict bulldoze me into a corner so I replied, "What were you doing there?"

"Business."

"Business?"

"Business," he repeated. "When times are tough I go there to see if I can make some extra coin."

"Like selling weed?"

Ignoring my question, he asked one of his own, "You weren't there doing business by any chance were you, Mike?"

"I don't sell drugs if that's what you mean."

"I'm not talking about drugs, bro. I'm talking about..." His gaze drifted to my crotch for a lingering moment before returning to my face. "You catch my drift?"

"Oh." My shock was delayed and I let out a second but louder, "Oh..."

"Cos I don't need any more competition. Pretty young pakeha boys like you are bad for business. You wouldn't be the first little punk in this neighbourhood who thought it was an easy way to make himself pocket money. And I like you, Mike, so I'd rather you and me not have ourselves a problem."

It suddenly dawned on me that the purpose of Damian's visit was to intimidate me. And it sort of did. He may not have had the muscles he once did but I was pretty sure the former gym bunny could still kick the shit out of me if he wanted to.

"Honestly, Damian, I just stopped off there for a piss. That's all."

"Are you sure about that?"

"Of course I'm bloody sure. You don't think I was actually there to..."

He took a couple more steps toward me, getting all in my space. His eyes were kinda hooded and locked onto my mouth when he said, "To make money with your dicksucker."

"I wasn't. I'm not that sort of person." I cringed at how that came out. "Sorry. No offense."

"I don't suck dick because I like the taste of it. It's just an easy way to make a buck."

A cauldron of awkward tension bubbled around the room and I was desperate to end the silence so I said the first thing that popped into my head. "What do you charge?" Probably not the best brain fart I'd ever had in my life.

Damian curled his upper lip and stared into my eyes. "How come you're so fucking interested in my rates if you're not a competitor?"

"Sorry, man. I'm just curious."

He eyed me stiffly before giving an answer. "Let's just say I make the desirable affordable."

I couldn't tell if that was supposed to be a joke or misplaced arrogance talking. Either way I knew it was Damian being cagey. I actually wondered if he was embarrassed, like he suddenly realised his impromptu visit to intimidate me hadn't been warranted.

"A lot of it depends on my mood and who the guy is," Damian clarified. "If it's some old crusty bastard then he gets charged ugly tax."

The laugh I let out sounded like a nervous twitch. "Sounds fair."

"And it ain't like I'm there cruising all the time. I only saw you that day cos I'd gone to make sure my number was still on the wall in the toilets. That's how I roll. Make them call me and meet somewhere else less risky. I might be down on my luck but even I don't want to get a reputation as a Hickford Homo. Fuck that for a joke."

I couldn't decide if this meant Damian wasn't as drug-fucked as I had assumed or if even someone constantly drifting in and out of homelessness was scared of the reputation that came with being known as a Hickford Homo.

"You ain't gonna tell no one about this?" His gruffness had disappeared and now he looked almost pleading. "If my ex found out she'd stop letting me see my kids. Bitch barely lets me spend any time with them as it is."

"Nar, man. I won't say anything."

"Cheers, Mike. And sorry for thinking you were...you know."

"No worries."

"I should have known based on where you walked into that's not what you were doing, but I just assumed the worst."

"What do you mean, where I walked into?"

"You wandered into the pig pen. That's where the heavy duty shit goes down."

"That probably explains why some freak wandered over to watch me take a piss."

Amusement fanned fine creases at the corners of his eyes. "You're lucky it didn't go any further than that. Had it been much later in the day then you might have found yourself in a sticky situation."

"Such as?"

"A cute boy like you would have been forced to be the pig."

"The pig?"

"That bush area where you went is where anything goes. There's usually one or two horny faggots on the ground begging for some dick. Anyone can fuck them. It's where the most desperate go to get their rocks off. Pigs don't say no to any cock. Chances are that's what you pissed on. A pig who had got there bright and early."

"Holy shit."

"Yeah. It can get pretty fucking messy in that spot. Sometimes I go up there to watch just for a laugh."

"It's funny?"

"It can be. One time the pig actually squealed like a pig. Like that redneck movie where they rape the fat dude? It was fucking hilarious." Damian made some oinking noises then started sniggering. "I also watched a dude get fisted there once. That was intense."

"Oh my god."

"The pig was fine. Most of them are older and have worn out cunts anyway."

"So you've actually..."

"Fucked one of them?"

"Yeah?"

"I've done it a few times." Damian scratched himself through his boxers, the movement giving away the outline of his dick. "A couple of my regulars get off on watching me in action. They say my fuck style is a work of art."

That was an overshare I didn't need to know but I humoured him with a smile.

"Speaking of pigs." Damian raised his arms in a stretch, showing off the thick hair in his armpits. "Is it all good if I go take that shower now? I smell kind of rank."

"Of course. Water takes a while to heat up, but it gets really hot so be careful. Towels are under the sink."

"Thanks. I'll try not to melt my flesh off." He rifled through his backpack, pulling out a change of clothes and a baggie containing a toothbrush and cheap deodorant.

As he strolled down the hallway, my gaze burned into the seat of those cheap silk boxers he wore. I don't think I had ever considered Damian in a sexual light before but knowing that for the right price I could see those boxers come off did make my heart beat a little faster. He may not have had the muscular physique of days gone by but he wasn't in bad shape, his legs still toned and his shoulders broad.

I felt the blood rush out of every other inch of my body and into my crotch. Rather than do something stupid, like follow Damian to the shower and ask him how much he'd charge to lick my asshole, I went and checked my wallet to make sure he hadn't stolen my winning ticket.

Chapter 6

SOMETIME AFTER TWO in the morning I heard banging and scratching at the front door. Thinking I was about to be the victim of a home invasion, I fetched an old cricket bat out of my closet and made my way to the front of the house. With the bat raised in one hand over my shoulder, and summoning my best *don't-fuck-with-me* face, I pulled open the door and was ready to scream "Get the fuck off my property!" when I saw Gavin standing there fumbling with a set of keys.

He wasn't wearing any shoes and his t-shirt was on backwards and inside out. By his crossed-eyes, crooked smile and wavering hand holding the wrong key, I could determine he was drunk. His car was nowhere in sight, so at least he'd had enough sense to walk home and not drive.

He stumbled past me into the living room and tumbled to the sofa. The muscles in his face were softened by his drunken state, mouth sagging like he was in a sulk.

"I thought you were staying at Fiona's house tonight?" It was both a question and a statement.

"That was the plan."

"So...what happened?"

"I don't know."

I rolled my eyes. "Don't pull the I don't know card."

"…"

"Don't pull the silence either." I stared accusingly. "Did you have a fight?"

"More like a disagreement."

"But it was bad enough to leave?"

"Yep."

Then, as if in slow motion, I watched Gavin's drunken composure morph into a drunken ramble. "I was going to stay over but the bitch is crazy. Crazy with a capital psycho." His hands flew up wildly in the air. "If your mother was captain of the crazies then Fiona's the fucking general of the army."

No disagreement from me.

"I don't care how pretty she is," Gavin slurred, "there's no fucking way I'm doing what she asked me to do."

"What did she ask you to do?"

"What didn't she ask more like it." He took a deep breath and huffed his fringe back in place. "That woman is full of demands. Thinks she can get away with it too."

I went to the kitchen to make some coffee. He went on as I knew he would. Drunks do that a lot. Especially a drunk Gavin.

When I returned with the coffees he'd calmed down and was back to drunken composure, irritated but not fiery. We didn't speak for a while, just sat together on the couch. I figured he'd tell me when and if he was ready.

"Has Jockey ever said much about what dating Fiona was like?" Gavin asked.

"Not for ages. But he used to go on about her all the time. Anyone would have thought he was the first dude in the world who ever had a girlfriend."

Gavin laughed, but I could tell it was forced. "Did he say anything specific...like any habits or demands she'd make?"

"I'm not following."

Gavin looked like he was blushing. "Never mind."

"Nar, what is it?"

"It's just that...and I'm not complaining, but Fiona's quite the vixen in the bedroom, if you catch my drift."

Oh boy. I had a suspicion where this was going. And so did my balls as they began to tingle. Starved of a morning wank, they were keen to hear some filth.

"So I just wondered if Jockey had ever said anything to you about that? Because I imagine she must have taught him a thing or two."

"He's said a couple things," I replied cryptically.

"Such as?"

"Just that she was pretty kinky."

"She's certainly fucking that," Gavin exclaimed. "That girl's got tricks I never even heard of. But again, not complaining."

"Then why do you want to know if Jockey has said anything?"

Gavin glanced around as if to make sure no one could overhear our conversation. "It's just that there's one thing she wants to do that I'm a bit iffy about. But she said if I do it she'll do whatever I want in return."

"What does she want you to do?"

He studied my face then shook his head. "Sorry. I probably shouldn't be telling you this stuff."

"That's never stopped you before."

"She wants us to have a threesome. With another bloke."

"Really?" I feigned surprise.

"Like, I'm an openminded sort of bloke. I even voted for the Greens once. But you gotta draw the line somewhere. And that line for me is sharing a bed with anyone who has an asshole hairier than mine."

"Maybe the guy shaves it?"

"Very funny, Mikey."

"I thought so."

"How hairy the guy's ass is isn't exactly the issue. The point is I'm not a shirt lifter." He clasped a hand over his mouth and burped. "Anyway, I don't have to worry about it. I told her we're through."

I nodded sympathetically while smiling with delight on the inside. It was about time he saw through Fiona. The woman was trouble. Of that I was sure.

"Anyway, enough about my love life," Gavin said. "How was your night?"

I contemplated telling him about my winning scratchie ticket but decided I'd rather tell him while he was sober. "It was alright. A bit of Netflix. A bit of chill."

Gavin sipped his coffee. He was studying me, and I noticed a small smile behind the rim of the coffee mug. "Did your sexy vampire come over by any chance? Did she give you any new puncture wounds?"

I shook my head, telling him, "No sexy vampire visited here tonight."

"I bet she did. You can tell me. I don't mind. As long as ya wrapping up you can have her over whenever you like."

"The only person who visited while you were out was Damian Takarangi. He came to ask if he could use our shower."

Gavin sat back a bit as if I'd let out a stinky fart. "I hope you told the fucking deadbeat to piss off."

"Nar, Damian's alright."

"No he's not." Gavin shook his head firmly. "That jobless piece of rangi brown shit is bad news. Always has been." Gavin saw the look I gave him. "What? I can say it. I'm brown too." He flashed one of his bare arms at me as if it were an identity card. "It's part of my indigenous rights I'll have you know."

"You're not that brown."

"I'm brown enough not to get sunburned by a lightbulb, unlike the melanin-challenged member of this family."

I laughed and smiled, pleased to hear him refer to us as a family.

"What did Damian do to rub you the wrong way so much?" I asked. "Aside from not having a job."

"To be honest, him not having a job doesn't bother me so much. It's the fact he's out there getting girls pregnant when he can't even afford to pay child support to the first two he had."

"Damian has kids to other women? But I thought he only had kids with Stacy."

"He has at least seven other kids so I've been told. Maybe more." Gavin took a sip on his coffee. "I tell ya, you learn all the gossip if you go to the local tavern enough. They all call Damian slut nuts down there."

"Slut nuts." I snorted.

"If the shoe fits."

"Gossip isn't always true, Gavin."

"This gossip is. And did you know he was in court again last month for assault?"

"Bullshit. Damian's not violent." As soon as I said that I wasn't sure I entirely believed it. Not after the aggro vibe he'd come here with earlier.

"The cunt was a fucking bouncer back in the day," Gavin said far too loudly. "Violence was his bread and butter. Why do you think he keeps getting hidings so fucking often? Because he keeps picking fights he can't win anymore."

"Who did he assault?"

"Some guy that was living in the same boarding house as him. And it's not the first time Damian's assaulted someone he lives with. Why do you think he keeps ending up homeless?"

"Because he has a drug habit he spends his rent money on."

"I'm sure that doesn't help but it's not the main reason he keeps getting booted out of places. I hear now that he's living in a campground somewhere."

"Yeah. Apparently."

"Trent's little brother went to school with him. Marshall said Damian used to be a big-time bully, beating the shit out of all the younger kids. He's always been a slimeball. I know I've always thought so."

"Was that before or after you heard this gossip?"

"Before," Gavin said seriously. "You know my spidey senses can tell who's good and who's bad."

"And what are your spidey senses telling you about Fiona after tonight?"

Gavin pondered the question, too drunk to detect my selfish motivation for asking it. Finally, he answered with music to my ears, "To stay the hell away."

Chapter 7

I AWOKE THE FOLLOWING morning to the sound of vomiting. Following the echo of violent heaving, I found seventy inches of pale brown muscle hung over the toilet. Half-naked in just a pair of threadbare briefs, Gavin's head was poked inside the toilet bowl. When he peered up at me, his bloodshot eyes made me wince in sympathy. He looked helpless, but also kind of adorable.

"Sorry if I woke you," he said in a voice so weak I could barely distinguish the words. "I think I might be a little hung over."

"More than just a little by the looks." My gaze wandered over his back which was covered in red scratch marks; clearly last night there had been fucking before the fighting. "Did you want me to get you some water or anything?"

"Yes, please. And some"—in place of his next word came a stream of vomit. He clutched the rim of the toilet, speckled with pubic hairs and splotches of yellow grime, his head disappearing into the bowl. Gags and whimpers echoed off the porcelain.

I fetched him the requested glass of water and some paracetamol—which I assumed had been the word lost to his spew. He downed both pills as if he'd just swallowed poison. Nodding his thanks, he handed me back the glass and asked me to bring him his phone.

"Why do you need your phone?"

"I've gotta call Trent. I need him to give me a lift to go get my car."

"I can go get it for you."

"But Fiona lives halfway across town. It's a long way to walk."

"I don't mind," I said a bit too eagerly. "I've got the day off work so it's not like I haven't got the time."

"You're a legend, Mikey. Thank you."

"You don't mind if I borrow the car for the day then after I pick it up?"

"Fine by me. As long as I can stay here and die in peace then I don't care." He muttered something under his breath, coughed and puked again.

So much for the Panadol.

When he was done he sat staring into the bowl. Then he rocked back on his heels, raised his face to the ceiling, his eyes full of regret.

"Better?"

He nodded and smiled weakly and leaned back on his heels again. He looked pissed off. I didn't blame him. Puking was like getting violated by your own body.

I dug around in the bathroom cabinet, through curled-up tubes of toothpaste and two gnarly toothbrushes and found a bottle of blue Listerine with an eighth of an inch left in the bottom. I unscrewed the cap and handed it to him. He took it, swished half-heartedly, spat in the toilet, flushed.

"Thanks," he said, squinting now. He closed the lid and put his hands on it to stand up. Staggering slowly, he went and rinsed his hands under the tap. He threw a palmful of water at his vomit-stained face then slunk back to his room, a hand digging around the back of his undies while he gave his ass a good scratch.

Classy guy, I thought with a smile.

Gavin may have been a bit of a slob but he was my slob and I wasn't about to let Fiona get her claws back into him now that he'd finally come to his senses. Which meant one long-ass hike to get his car so he didn't have a chance to see her and patch things up.

FOR THE FIRST EIGHT years of my life it had just been me and my mum. I liked it that way, and was never happy when she started dating someone. Even though I had just been a young child I'd always sort of known when a new man—or the occasional woman—entered our lives that they wouldn't be around for long. Mum was quick to bore of people, taking the good time without committing for a long time.

Until she met Gavin.

Gavin Masters was only in his mid-twenties at the time and worked at the local freezing works. The handsome part-Māori man was athletic, good-natured, funny as you like, and worshipped the ground my mother walked on.

I hated the guy instantly.

But he swept Mum off her feet— and way too easily, I might add. A few dinner dates at lousy restaurants and flowers sent to her work and suddenly she was "in love." I couldn't believe it happened so fast. Just a few months later we moved in with the guy.

Gavin was thrilled to welcome Mum and me into his home, a small but cute two-bedroom house on the edge of town in Moa Hill's Tamati Subdivision. Although it was considered one of the rougher neighbourhoods the house itself was a big upgrade from Mum's apartment we'd been living in, but I didn't let Gavin know how much I liked his house or that I was over the moon to finally live somewhere with a yard.

Granted, I was a sulky only child who was overly protective of his one parent and didn't like sharing her with others, although I was constantly forced to. This free spirit of hers often troubled a younger me, constantly worrying she might grow bored of me too, which may have made me clingier than I naturally was.

To my surprise I grew to love Gavin as much as Mum did. He didn't force the father role on me and I felt like we struck a healthy balance between him being my stepfather and my friend. I remember when I was ten Mum asking me if I wanted to start calling Gavin dad. I'd told her no and that he was 'just Gavin' to me. The truth is I had wanted to call him Dad quite desperately, to lay claim to him in some way, but had felt awkward about it, like maybe he wouldn't want me to. After all, it was Mum who'd asked me the question, not him.

Nowadays I cared for Gavin just as much as I had for mum. Maybe even more. And even though he was completely different to my free-spirited mother, and arguably cared about me much more than she ever did, I was still terrified of him doing what she had.

Growing tired of me.

Chapter 8

THE WALK TO FIONA'S took me nearly an hour, but it was a small sacrifice to make if it meant Gavin didn't have to come here to get the vehicle. He wasn't the sort of person to stay angry with anyone for long, his belief in 'never let the sun set on an argument' was as much a blessing as it was a curse. I worried that if he'd come to Fiona's on his own then he may have done something silly like go inside and patch things up with madam kink.

When I arrived at Fiona's house, I was relieved to find Gavin's beat-up Honda parked outside on the street. I'd been worried it might have been in the driveway and I'd be forced to go and knock on the door to let Fiona know I was just here to pick up the car. The last thing I wanted was to make small talk with her. It shouldn't have bothered me how she'd tried to rope Gavin into her twisted fantasies. After all, he was an adult and big enough to look after himself. But it still annoyed me. I'd always been protective of Gavin and that instinct had only increased after my mother had run off.

Speeding off in Gavin's car as if I'd just stolen it, I made my way out of town and onto the highway. I had no destination in mind, just drove aimlessly and enjoyed the sense of freedom that came from being on the open road. I entertained a little fantasy of cashing in my winning scratchie ticket and driving up to surprise

Brian. But there were several reasons why I couldn't embark on a spontaneous road trip; the main one being I couldn't be sure how pleased Brian would be to see me.

I did, however, decide to stop off at a small lotto store in the next town over to cash in my winning ticket. The woman behind the counter told me I was lucky it was only five-hundred I had won; anything more than that then I'd have had to approach Lotto's head office for my winnings. I don't know how winning less made me lucky but I could sort of see her point. I could also see the sour look on her face as she handed me my prize winnings, her smile crumpling under the effort as she told me, "You cleaned me out, love. Now I have to go top up the till's float."

I left the store with a smile on my face and my wallet the fattest it had ever been in its life. Knowing I had money to burn was exciting and I contemplated going on a shopping spree at the mall and blowing the lot on video games or new clothes. But I held off doing that, telling myself it would be wiser to enjoy the feeling of being rich a little longer.

I continued driving north along the coast, blasting music on the stereo while wind flew in the open window blowing my long hair back. The scenery slowly changed from farmland to forest as the highway narrowed and wove its way along the windy coast. The black sand beaches were rough and wild, the white-tipped waves crashing against the shoreline with violent beauty. This was a beautiful part of the country, remote and untouched, but it didn't change the fact I lived in the ass-end of nowhere. The remoteness heightened my sense of loneliness, reminding me how I lived at the bottom of the world, thousands of miles away from international relevancy. For a brief moment I almost understood why Mum had taken her chance to escape to Australia, abandoning the quietness of an at times mentally cruel paradise.

I managed to get as far north as the Waikato border, the region before Auckland. If I wanted I could be with Brian in just over a couple of hours. The temptation was strong but again I knew better. There would be no way I would make it home in time tomorrow for my early shift at work.

At the next rest area I pulled off the road and turned around to head back to Moa Hill. The drive back was far less freeing, my sense of adventure all but gone, that was until I found myself driving past Hickford Park—Moa Hill's infamous cruising spot. I tried convincing myself I'd driven this way for a scenic detour on my way home, but this scraggly, neglected park was not in a scenic part of town. No, the reason I'd come here honestly was to see if I could spot Mr Quayle's car. It had also been a Wednesday night two weeks ago when I'd seen his vehicle here and I guess I wanted to know if it had just been a coincidence that Brian's father had been parked in Moa Hill's most notorious cruising spot.

I drove past slowly, checking to see how many people were loitering about. There was a young mother pushing her son on the swing set, near them were two youths kicking a soccer ball about, and then standing over by the old fountain outside the long-abandoned tea rooms was the usual gaggle of teenaged delinquents smoking weed and trying their best to look thuggish. There was no sign of Mr Quayle's black Mercedes.

Of course he's not here. You were looking for scandal where there isn't any.

To be honest, I couldn't decide if I was relieved or disappointed. The part of me that looked up to the Quayles as the perfect family was certainly relieved, but the storyteller in me, the part that loved conjuring up dark mysteries, was a little disappointed.

Clearly the man had just parked here the other week without thinking and must have walked to the squash club—which I assumed was nearby.

I was about to turn around and head straight home for dinner, but just as I pulled over to make the U-turn I spotted the black Mercedes with its unmistakable number plate **Quayle** parked a block further down the road.

That doesn't mean anything. The squash club must be down there.

But I knew it wasn't. The only thing in that direction was a couple mechanic shops and an old woolshed used for indoor go-cart racing. Abandoning the U-turn, I made a sharp left into the domain's carpark area. The carpark was its own mini road that ran the length of the domain, sky-touching Norfolk pines dotted the perimeter. To the left the carpark was empty, but to the right was about five vehicles all parked close together. I turned towards the small cluster of cars but parked up about thirty metres away, wanting to be close but not too close.

Switching off the engine, I looked in the direction of the cars parked further along. Standing outside one of the vehicles was a tall and slender man with his hands planted on the roof of the car, his head lowered to talk to whoever it was inside the vehicle. It seemed innocent enough, but instinctively I knew it wasn't based on the baseball cap and sunglasses the man standing outside the car was wearing.

I felt like an idiot parked here, looking for drama I instinctively knew didn't exist. Even if the squash club wasn't nearby that didn't mean Mr Quayle didn't have a reason to be in this area. Maybe he used Hickford Park to practise for the triathlons he occasionally competed in, not realising he was cycling and running around a field littered with joints and jizz. He was certainly old enough to be out of the loop of what many younger folk knew to be a very seedy area.

But when I turned to look ahead and observe the domain again, I could see no sign of a ropey baby boomer puffing his way around the field. I did notice though that some of the teens by the fountain were beginning to head off, making their way home before the grassy field became a penis prairie for lovers of cock. The last shreds of daylight were still in the sky, telling me it was a similar hour to when I'd stopped off here last week to take a piss. That meant I was early.

Early for what? My inner voice scolded.

It wasn't as if I was going to get out of the car and hunt down a fuck. I wasn't *that* desperate. But I was nosey to see the sort of men who came here to get their rocks off. Maybe I'd see Damian loitering in the shadows, looking to make a few bucks. The thought of a straight man reduced to sucking cock for drug money should have made me wince in sympathy but instead I felt myself shiver with a dark curiosity. But I wasn't curious enough to get out of the car. Hell to the no on that one.

Right at that moment, as if mocking me on purpose, my bladder demanded a piss. I contemplated just starting the car again and driving home to use my own toilet, but that seemed an overreaction. Provided I didn't wander into the bushes again, or the pig pen as Damian had called it, then it was probably wiser to be a man and just take a piss in the actual toilet block. After all, that's what they were there for.

Focused on the goa of bladder relief, I got out the car and locked it, then trekked across the field towards the archaic toilet block about fifty metres away. As I got closer to my destination, the two youths who'd been playing soccer together were walking in my direction. I picked them to be about my age; bored teens in a boring town. The one holding the soccer ball was tall and dark-haired, nothing extraordinary about him other than a vast forehead and uncouth eyebrows. He was dressed head to toe in a blue Adidas tracksuit, looking a lot less cool than he probably thought he was. My gaze, however, was drawn to the cute shirtless blond boy walking beside him whose naked chest was dripping in sweat after their kick about. Rocking the cockiest of cocky swaggers, he sported shiny blond-haired legs curtained with swooshy basketball shorts, and a sensual mouth that would have looked right at home at the end of my cock.

I imagined the pair as a comedic duo, one bringing the goofy the other the sex appeal: Blondie and Lurch.

"You don't wanna stay here much longer, bro," said Lurch. "The Hickford Homos will be here shortly."

It wasn't said with malice, just a genuine heads-up that shit was about to change around here. Probably in just a matter of minutes.

I nodded my head in thanks and kept on walking, relieved to know they didn't just assume I was one of the Hickford Homos. *And I'm not*, I reminded myself. *I'm just a guy who needs a piss...and who is curious to see if his best friend's father is a closet case.*

The toilet block was architecturally gorgeous, two small domes jutting up from the old concrete structure below. I recalled reading an article in the local paper about how Hickford Park had once been the jewel in Moa Hill's crown, but that was almost a century ago, now it was more like a thorn in its side.

I pulled open the men's room door. It groaned as if in protest, and I walked inside to the restroom. Thankfully there was a light on, as dim as it was, casting a faint yellow glow through the restroom. I glanced around my surroundings taking in the grimy mirrors that lined the walls and the broken coloured tiles on the floor. Once upon a time this space would have been sparkling and ornate but now it was just creepy. My storyteller brain began conjuring up images of violence and sex, and the ghosts of a time gone by.

To my right was a row of stalls, to my left a bank of old-fashioned urinals. At the drain of each urinal, bright pink deodorizer cakes barely did their job of masking the stench of stale piss. Rather than risk getting caught standing in the open at one of the urinals, I chose to be a pussy and use one of the stalls for some privacy.

But each of the four stalls had a hole in the wall. I knew what these holes were used for, and anyone who didn't was clearly told by little messages written above each hole that said ***put your dick in here***. One of these cock-guiding messages though had been written over in bold red letters ***AIDS HURTS SINNERS!***

Deciding I didn't want to piss alongside far-right preaching, I opted to use the stall right at the end. It also meant I only had to worry about being spied on from one side as opposed to two. But that seemed unlikely since the eerie quiet told me I was the only person in the restroom.

Before unzipping my jeans to take a piss, I stopped to admire the mosaic of graffiti extending from top to bottom of the stall wall. It was of every size, shape and colour; promises of a good time mingled with racist and homophobic slurs. Evidently the young deadbeats who loitered at the park in the daytime liked to express themselves while they answered the call of nature. I chuckled at some of the juvenile scrawling before my attention gravitated to the defiled wall's centrepiece—a throbbing twelve-inch cock spurting cum bullets halfway across the stall wall.

The artist had even gone to the effort of adding a pair of oversized nuts with wiry pubic hair. I ran my eyes up and down the vulgar image, soaking up its provocative fascination, until my gaze became fixed on a set of scrawled words that had been scratched on the wall underneath the spurting member in the same bold, black ink. They read: ***R U looking 4 good time$? Young hot str8 Maori. Big dick. Text me on 025987789. No farking time wasters. I only meet for $$$!***

Feeling dizzy and light-headed, I instinctively knew whose number I was staring at. It was debatable just how 'young and hot' Damian Takarangi was but my guess was at twenty-nine he was probably much younger and hotter than the men who text him.

Blood rushed to the space between my legs while adrenaline pulsed through my body. Why was I so hot and bothered by Damian's ad? Surely it was just a case of thrills at seeing someone flaunt the rules so flagrantly. I willed my cock to calm down and finally got around to taking the piss I'd come in here for.

Finished with my business, I zipped my jeans up and left the cubicle. Standing before the washbasin, I ran cold water over my hands and face, trying to get my composure back. I had to will all of that stimulation away, get back to Gavin's car and keep an eye out for Mr Quayle. Just as I was about to leave, I heard the sound of muffled voices standing outside the restroom.

"How much?" said an older man's voice that sounded way too familiar for my liking.

A beat of silence was followed with:

"If you wanna suck me off, it'll be twenty bucks. I'll fuck you for thirty. For fifty, you can fuck me." This voice was much, much younger. "But you'd better be quick. I haven't got long."

Without even laying eyes on the owner of the young voice, I could still tell by his brusque tone that his natural habit would be to chase girls at the weekend with his mates rather than look for kicks in men's toilets.

"If you'd be up for it... I'd rather like to rim you."

The young voice replied, matter-of-factly, "That'll be twenty, then. Same as sucking. But no bitching about how dirty I am. I ain't showered since this morning."

"That just means you'll be even tastier." The older voice then let out a throaty chuckle and my stomach twisted. It was Mr Quayle. I was fucking sure of it.

Fuck! Fuck! Fuck!

I ran in lopsided circles like a headless chicken, looking for an escape route that didn't involve walking past my best friend's father who was about to pay someone for sex in a public toilet. When I heard them begin to open the door, I quickly dashed into the end cubicle again.

Not even a second later, the rusty entrance door squeaked open and two sets of footsteps approached the cubicles.

"Take your pick," said the younger voice.

"How about that one," replied Mr Quayle, or who I assumed was Mr Quayle. "I'd quite like us to have an audience."

"I don't give a fuck as long as you've got the cash."

I wondered what the heck they were on about until I heard the door of the cubicle next to mine open up. My body flung back against the opposite wall, clinging to it as if someone had pointed a gun to my head. I was terrified one of them might kneel down and peep through. Squinting through just one open eye, I watched as a pair of young sweat-glistening legs appeared, covered in a down of blond hairs and curtained with swooshy basketball shorts

It's Blondie!

I wondered if his tall friend had any idea he was mates with a bog-cruising rent boy. Blondie moved forward to make room for his client and that's when I saw long hairy legs on display in just a pair of skimpy black gym shorts. Relief swept through me. It wasn't Mr Quayle, it was the man I'd seen talking to someone in the carpark.

The youth turned around to face the older man and said, "You can rim me and wank yourself off, but that's it. No rubbing your cock up and down my ass, no spunking up against my ass... no nothing unless you happen to find a bit more cash."

The client handed him a twenty dollar note which the boy crumpled into a ball stuffed inside the pocket of his basketball shorts. Then he turned around to face the toilet and hitched his shorts down. He was wearing blue and purple stripy boxer briefs which he started to pull down but the older man stopped him.

"Let me just admire those lovely undies a little longer." The voice sounded so similar to Brian's father but I put it down to men of a certain age sounding the same. "You look so good in them."

"I haven't got long, remember?" the boy complained.

"Don't worry my sweet boy. If we run over time then I can pay extra."

"You fucking better." I'm sure that was supposed to sound like a threat but it came out boyish and weak, revealing that he probably didn't possess the strength to back up his tough talk.

From where I stood, I had the perfect view of Blondie's ass and backs of his thighs. His bum looked very attractive in his boxer briefs. The tops of his legs, just below the hemline, were quite hairy with a more dense growth on the inside of his thighs leading upwards towards his crack. This was going to be so fucking hot...

But I shouldn't be here. Now is the time to leave.

But I was glued to the spot I stood, my eyes feasting on the sexy boy's underpants.

A pair of older hands, smaller with well-kept nails, came forward and slowly tugged the boy's briefs down his legs. The youth's muscular buttocks were pert and squat, making his crack quite short and distinctly masculine in appearance. The skin was blemish free, and the only hair was a dusting of light blond fuzz. It was a divine sight and I found myself eager to watch the older man get his face stuck between such magnificent cheeks.

Those mature hands parted the boy's cheeks, the man's furry arm obstructing my view. I dared to lean forward to get a better look and that's when I saw the boy's crack was much harrier than I'd expected. I could tell he hadn't been lying about not showering today. His crack appeared moist with sweat and clogged with smells. A couple bits of dried toilet paper clung to the scraggly brown hairs around his asshole. I was grossed out at the thought of someone licking out an unwashed shithole but at the same time my cock pulsed with desire to see it done.

"That's a beautiful asshole you have there," the man said as he stroked a finger down the boy's crack. "I bet its very fuckable too."

"If you pay me fifty then you can find out."

Rather than respond, the older man leaned forward and licked the entire length of the boy's hair-lined crack, pressing in deep over the boy's hole. The youth and I let out a moan at the same time, but for very different reasons.

The older man's cap and sunglasses were gone and I now knew I had been right in the first place. It was Mr Quayle!

My yelp of shock did not go unnoticed.

"Are you enjoying the show, friend?" Mr Quayle said. He spoke the words directly into Blondie's butthole but they were aimed at me.

Had he turned to look then he would have seen me, but thankfully Rowan Quayle's face remained buried in the teen's backside and he resumed licking the unwashed shitter. I was torn between fear and lust, a need to run but a desire to stay.

The more Brian's father licked, the louder the teens moans became. I could tell the boy was doing his best to keep quiet, probably embarrassed to let us know how much he was enjoying being licked out by a much older man. He was fighting a losing battle though and pretty soon he was spreading his legs and pushing his ass back into Mr Quayle's face, begging for that tongue to dig deeper.

A hot, pulsating pleasure seethed through my cock and my balls tingled as I watched Mr Quayle tongue-fuck the boy's hole. While Blondie struggled to keep quiet, Brian's father ate that dirty ass so ravenously that his wet slurping was practically deafening.

I was fascinated. Was that how I had sounded at the beach that night? Just a wriggling mound of flesh begging to be tongue-fucked? I was also weirdly fascinated knowing who the man was licking this barely legal shitter. My best friend's father! A man who I'd always associated with the perfect marriage and a white picket fence. But here he was kneeling on a piss-stained floor while he ate out a boy his own son's age.

As disgusted as I was, I could not deny there was a delightful perversion to witnessing such an immoral act. It was so wrong and dirty which was probably why I found it so sexy. Provided the old coot never laid a hand on me I was more than happy to watch him corrupt another young person's innocence.

"If I had a rubber I'd fuck you so hard," Mr Quayle breathed into the boy's asshole, his hands running up and down Blondie's sweat-glistening legs. "But this feels pretty good."

"You don't need a rubber," the boy said. "For sixty you can fuck me raw."

"You dirty boy." Mr Quayle chuckled darkly. "Do you like men my age coming inside you?"

"Better in me than on me," the boy grunted. "That way my girlfriend won't see it."

There was the confirmation. He was indeed straight, just tolerating the affection of older men to make a quick buck.

Rather than take the teen up on his bareback offer, Brian's father parted the boy's buttocks again and admired the young spit-soaked asshole. He traced a finger around the rim of the youth's asshole then, without asking, he rammed a finger inside.

The boy jolted and hissed. "I didn't say you could do that!"

Rowan Quayle ignored the warning he'd just been given and pushed his finger in deeper, wiggling it around the moist channel of Blondie's anus. He must have touched the boy's prostate or something because Blondie let out a pleasurable moan and backed up onto the older man's bony finger.

"You like that, Stryder?"

Stryder—if that was even his real name—answered with a shuddering moan.

Rowan's middle finger joined his index finger, the digits sliding deep into Stryder's asshole. "There's still a lot of give to these pretty lips of yours," he said. "That tells me you must be very popular."

"Sort of."

"More than sort of, dear boy." Mr Quayle wriggled his fingers some more, eliciting another shaky moan from his gay for pay treat. A third finger was added, taking up the slack. To my astonishment, Brian's father added a fourth, and this must have been the kid's limit.

"Okay, that's enough, dude," Stryder grunted through clenched teeth.

"Have you ever been fisted?"

"Look, man, that's not what I agreed to." Trying to sound tough, and failing miserably. He had his shorts around his ankles and four fingers up his butt—how threatening did he expect to be, I wondered.

"I might want to renegotiate our terms." Mr Quayle chuckled. He applied a little more pressure, and Stryder's ass reluctantly swallowed another half inch.

"This...this isn't funny." Stryder was whimpering now. "I don't do that shit."

With a snort of contempt, Rowan retrieved his fingers and Stryder let out a relieved sigh. Rather than close back up like it should, the teen's ass just hung open, a loose gaping chasm rimmed by spit-drenched ass hairs. This Stryder kid may have been straight but he'd trained his asshole to crave cock, its loose lips pouting like it was desperate for a feed. I wondered how long he had been whoring himself out at this park.

Too long and too frequently by the looks.

Before Stryder's asshole had a chance to close properly, Mr Quayle dove in and tongue-fucked the gape, slurping up the boy's juices. The rimming must have gone on for another five minutes and I could feel my briefs becoming soaked with precum. I was about to drop my pants and have a wank while I watched them, but I quickly let go of my zipper when I saw Mr Quayle lower his face to the floor.

"I like your sneakers, neighbour. You must be quite young. How old are you?"

My jaw stiffened and my legs turned to cement. I'd been so concerned about him spotting me through the glory hole that I hadn't considered the prospect of him looking under the stall wall.

"All the sexy young boys like to wear those sorts of shoes. My son has a pair just like them." Mr Quayle reached under the partition and stroked the top of my left shoe; his breathing became dark and predatory. "I used to sneak into his room, naked, and sniff them when he wasn't home. I like to lay on his bed while I do it and rub my balls on his pillows."

You sick fuck!

I couldn't comprehend how this man I had known for years, a loving husband and father, could sniff his own son's stinky sneakers. And get off on it!

"This ain't a confessional, old man," Stryder snapped impatiently. "Hurry up and finish rimming me so I can go meet my girl."

Rather than be offended, Mr Quayle chuckled warmly and let go of my foot. "How about we do this instead. I'll pay you thirty dollars to suck off our neighbour with the cool shoes in the next stall. And make sure you swallow."

"Deal."

I dared to aim my gaze back to the glory hole and saw Stryder hitching his shorts back up. He turned around with his greedy hand waiting for payment. I knew this was the moment I needed to make a run for it but just as I turned towards the door I heard

Stryder say, "Hello you." With a sense of dread, I turned back to see that the spunky blond was on his knees, his smirking face looking right at me through the glory hole.

I stood there like a stunned rabbit.

"You're new at this, aren't you, bro?" The boy's voice was a whisper, yet it crackled with an energy and vitality that made my spine tingle and my butthole quiver.

I tried to answer, but all that came out was a small croak. His face looked so boyish and innocent, but his hazel eyes revealed a depth of experience.

"Don't worry. I'm cool. You're safe with me." He smiled at me and for a moment I genuinely thought he found me attractive

Until...

"Come on, bro. Slip it through the hole. I want that extra thirty bucks."

I stared at those sensual lips of his, imagining how good they would feel wrapped around my cock. And he was cute. Very cute.

But I don't want to become a Hickford Homo.

Just as quickly as that thought popped into my head it was smacked down by another one.

But you're only a Hickford Homo if you get caught and end up on the internet.

I'll confess, there was a part of me that was repulsed by the fact that I was actually considering shoving my cock through that hole in order to feed the mouth of a rent boy on the other side.

At the same time, I'd never been so aroused.

I don't know if it was my curiosity, the anonymity of it all, or that I was turned on by the perverted seediness that permeated the bathroom. Whatever the reason, I knew somehow this was a rite of passage for me. It was something I had to do, and no matter how disgusting it might have appeared to someone else—including the rational side of me—this was how it had to be. It was what I needed to do.

As if watching myself through someone else's eyes, I unzipped my jeans and stepped up to the hole and shoved my dick through as far as I could. I almost gasped as I pressed my abdomen tight against the cold surface of the dividing wall.

I waited for the boy's lips but he appeared to be hesitating. Was something wrong? Was my dick not up to standard. I began to feel like a fool, that I'd been had by a cheap whore and my best friend's father. I was about to pull back when I heard Mr Quayle say, "Enjoy my generosity, neighbour. Remember, this one's on me."

Then a hot, moist mouth wrapped itself around my cock, and I really did gasp. "ohh fuck," I whispered, my voice too scrambled to be recognisable.

I heard Mr Quale leave the stall so me and blondie could be alone. He may have been young but damn this boy knew how to suck a dick. He was even better at it than Jockey, his tongue digging into my piss slit like he was trying to dig out every drop of precum brewed from watching him get rimmed.

All this was wordless, the only sound the hiss and gasping of our breaths, the wet slurping of his mouth, and the thumping of my heart. Not that either of us had much to say to each other.

Feeling safe now that it was just the two of us, I dared to ask, "Can you lick my balls? Suck on them a bit."

Deft fingers scooped my nuts through the hole and my young cocksucker mouthed the sweat off of my balls before returning his talented tongue to my cock and deepthroating me. The sensation that gripped me shut everything out but the feeling of hot wetness. All I could focus on was the pleasure coursing through my body.

It didn't matter this was someone who sold his body for money, or that it was happening inside public toilets, this was the sort of sexual pleasure I missed; a weaker male at the end of *my* knob, not the other way around.

I don't know how much longer I lasted. Perhaps a minute. Maybe two. All I know is that it was all over far too soon, and I came far more quickly than I would have liked.

You deserve a medal for your blowjob skills!

The thought echoed through me even as I whimpered and moaned. I tried to hang on to something, to keep from falling, but my knees grew weak, and I slipped to the floor, forehead pressed against the stall.

I heard Blondie smacking his lips and realized he was savouring my load. The thought of it actually thrilled me, and I wondered if I should ask him if he'd be keen to meet up sometime somewhere else. The fact I'd have to pay him was a downer but it would be worth it to feel his mouth on me again.

Still on my knees, as if lost in prayer, I felt something hot hit the top of my head. I pulled away and saw a girthy cock poking through the glory hole.

You cheeky fucker, I thought with a smile.

Had it been nearly any other guy I would have left his dick hanging but I knew essentially this was a freebie. My new friend was rewarding me. Maybe I was one of the few males he actually found attractive? Maybe I wouldn't have to pay for it.

Spurred on by an inflated ego, I opened my mouth, closed my eyes, and began to suck. Within minutes, something clanged against the wall. My young lover grunted and came in my mouth without warning. He was bittersweet with an acrid aftertaste. It didn't taste very nice if I'm being honest, but because he'd swallowed me I was determined to return the favour.

He gave a huge sigh, then pulled his cock from my mouth. Feeling a bit bashful, but also excited, I exited the stall to meet up with Blondie over by the hand basins.

"Thank you for that," I said while I washed my hands. "That was fucking awesome."

The door to his stall opened and in the reflection of the mirror I was horrified by what I saw.

"Michael?" My name tumbled out of Mr Quayle's shocked mouth.

Everything inside me heated at the familiarity of my name on the older man's lips. I spun around and we stared at one another for a lingering moment, each of us looking like we could faint on the spot. Finally my fight or flight instinct kicked in.

I chose flight.

THE WHOLE DRIVE HOME I couldn't stop spitting, desperate to get the taste of Mr Quayle's jizz out of my mouth. I felt dirty. So very, very dirty. I'd just sucked the cock of an old man. Sixty fucking years old to be precise! I felt sick, and I was very tempted to pull over and stick a finger down my throat so I could throw up his sperm, but I needed to get home. I needed to be with Gavin.

He'd make me feel better. I couldn't tell him what I'd just done but I knew just being near him would make everything okay.

Not only was I disgusted with myself, I was disgusted at Mr Quayle for lying. Clearly he'd paid the boy his money and they'd swapped places. The horny old coot probably thought he'd just scored himself a free dick to suck, like some sort of two-for one special. In a way the joke was also on him because he'd just had sexual relations with his son's best friend.

But him feeling shit doesn't mean I feel any better.

I was in such a rush to see my stepfather that when I got inside the house, I bypassed the bathroom and went straight to his bedroom. I barged in without knocking, hoping he'd had enough time to recover from his hangover. But I came to an abrupt halt when I saw what was going on. Gavin was on his back on the bed, naked. Sitting on top of him, her back to me, was Fiona. Her long blonde hair was bouncing against her back as she rode Gavin vigorously.

"Hey," I said, unable to stop myself before it came out.

Gavin looked up, his eyes dreamy from whatever paradise was wrapped around his cock. When he saw me, he smiled as if having me show up while he was in the middle of having sex wasn't weird. That's when I registered the stench of pot and realised the fucker was stoned. Fiona turned around and looked at me. Her large breasts, the nipples red like her painted nails, jiggled softly as she continued what she was doing.

"Mike!" Gavin said, his shock finally arriving. "Kinda busy here, matey."

"Hi," Fiona said breathlessly, giving a little wave of her fingers. I could see Gavin's balls between his spread legs, and every time Fiona raised herself up, several inches of his shaft slid out of her.

"S-Sorry," I stuttered, trying not to look at Fiona's breasts. I retreated from the room, shutting the door before I could see anything else.

Chapter 9

MY PHONE'S ALARM CLAWED at my ears, dragging me to consciousness. Bleary-eyed and gummy-mouthed; my jaw hurt, as though I'd been clenching it all night. I silenced my tormentor with a slap, and slowly rubbed my face.

The next thing to rub my face was Jockey's underwear which I'd stashed under the pillow following my bedtime wank the night before. I was still hooked on the putrid things, the musky smell of his ball sweat getting me high and hard each time I came into contact with them. They'd gotten extra use last night as I had sucked on the dry cum stains, desperately trying to replace the smell and taste of Mr Quayle's sex with Jockey's.

Perhaps that was the one good thing to come out of my shameful experience with Brian's father. I knew now I had taken Jockey for granted. It was time we made a new arrangement. One that saw us on equal terms. We could suck and fuck each other, and it didn't just have to be on Fridays. It could be any day of the week. I wondered now if that was what he'd secretly wanted all along. The whole *'you can be my faggot'* nonsense was just a ploy to get me to meet him halfway.

I had to admit that Jockey had been pretty patient with me. For two years he never once complained about being the one on his knees doing all the work while I just stood there pissing jizz into his mouth. This compromise was well overdue, as was an apology from me.

When I'd finished masturbating with his dirty undies, I put them down before grabbing my phone. I typed out a quick message that I assumed would make his day.

Hey man. I've been thinking and maybe it's time we make Friday nights a bit more fun for both of us. We can take turns doing it IYKWIM. I'm sorry for taking you for granted. It won't happen again.

I was happy enough with what it said. It got the point across without being blatant. Heaven forbid the dopey fuck put his phone down on a worksite and one of his workmates saw messages from me talking about sucking Jockey's cock. More importantly the text allowed me to sound like I was the boss, which I was really. That's how our friendship had always worked.

After a quick shower, I made my way into the kitchen where I found a mug of steaming hot coffee and a plate of toast waiting for me at the table. I looked over at Gavin who sat at the other end of the table with a greasy smile on his face. "I made you breakfast," he said. "And I put the vegemite on extra thick just the way you like."

"Why did you make me breakfast?" I asked warily as I sat down in front of the food. "It's not my birthday."

"I know but I just wanted to say thank you for you going to get my car for me yesterday. And I suppose it's also a bit of a sorry for what you walked in on."

"That's probably more my fault for not knocking."

"That's true," he agreed far too easily. "But I'm just hoping you don't end up scarred for life."

"Don't worry, I've seen way worse on the internet. But you're right, geriatric sex isn't pretty."

Gavin laughed. "I'm not even middle-aged yet ya cheeky shit."

It was nice of him to make me breakfast but I still wasn't pleased with him for getting back with Fiona. What happened to his spidey senses, huh? One look at her tits and the weak-willed bastard was back to chasing her like she was the last woman on earth. Adding to my annoyance with my stepfather was how bloody noisy he and Fiona had been last night. Their rowdy makeup sex consisted of several rounds that went late into the night, slaps and grunts coming through the thin walls separating our bedrooms. I don't think I managed to get to sleep until after midnight when I finally heard Fiona leave to go home.

"Eat up," Gavin said, pointing to the toast.

I didn't realise just how hungry I was until I took the first bite. "Is Fiona coming over tonight?" I mumbled through a mouthful of toast. I swallowed what I was chewing and washed it down with a slurp of coffee. "If she is then I'm buying earplugs. You two are too bloody noisy."

"Sorry about that. We were making up for lost time. And in answer to your question, you don't have to worry about getting earplugs just yet because I'm actually going to stay at her place tonight."

"But I thought her mother was going away today to visit relatives or some shit."

"Your point?"

"It means Fiona doesn't have a babysitter and her kids will be home."

"Yeah. She wants me to meet the little tykes."

"Gotcha."

"Gotcha?" Gavin eyeballed me. "What's that supposed to mean?"

"Nothing. It's just *gotcha*."

"You know, Mikey, you sure can be a stick in the mud sometimes."

"Why? Because I said gotcha?"

"No, it's that holier than thou look on ya face. Tells me that you don't approve of me meeting her children."

"It's none of my business what you two do."

"Even just the way you said that suggests you have an issue. What is it?" Like the proverbial dog with a bone, Gavin wasn't giving up until I had told him what I was thinking.

"Like I said," I blew on my tea and then took a small sip, "what you two do is none of my business."

"Just spit it out."

"Fine," I snapped. "I just wonder if it is wise to go play the role of overnight daddy with a woman you've only known a week."

"Two-and-a-half weeks."

"Even so, I just wonder if it's fair on the kids."

Gavin looked surprised. "Is that all?"

"What did you think I was gonna say?"

"I thought you were in a pissy about me dating your mate's ex-girlfriend."

"I don't give a shit about that. I don't even think Jockey would give a shit about that."

"Good." Gavin nodded to himself. "Cause I like Jockey, you know. He's a good egg. And I don't want to cause a rift between you two because of who I'm shagging."

"Cool."

"And just so you know, I get your point about the kids. I was overnight daddy to you once upon a time." Gavin waggled his eyebrows playfully. "But then I became your fulltime daddy."

"More like my fulltime Gavin."

"But I'm still ya daddy." His warm brown eyes lit with cheek.

"You're such a saddo."

"Saddo daddy. That's me."

"Well, if things work out with Fiona then you might get your wish to be called daddy. I think her kids are young enough to call you that."

"Nope. I'm fine with just being Gavin," he said. "I remember how awkward it was with you when I asked your mum to speak with you about it. She told me how you turned your nose up at the suggestion like she was trying to make you eat your vegetables."

The memory hit my brain like a torpedo. "You wanted me to call you dad? I thought that had been Mum's idea."

"Nar, it was mine. I was too embarrassed to ask you myself, and I was worried you'd feel like I was pressuring you so I got her to ask for me."

"I never knew that."

"Well... now ya do." Reaching up, he scratched his stubbly jaw, thinking. "But things happen the way they're meant to happen. I'm happy now just being Gavin. That's the sort of relationship we have and it works perfect. Don't you think?"

I nodded and forced out a smile, hiding my disappointment. I couldn't help but think a ten-year-old me had fucked up. All these years I could have had a dad, a real one in many respects, but I'd wrongly assumed Gavin had never really considered me his son. If I didn't have a truck-load of other bullshit to deal with right now then I would have scheduled myself a pity party over it.

When I'd finished my toast, I said, "I take it Fiona apologised then."

"She did."

"And she's promised to not make any more demands like she did the other night?"

The room became still. Gavin's gaze turned inward, and a fleeting, puzzled expression passed over his face as if whatever he was searching for had gone. I heard the frustration in his sigh and he dropped his eyes to the table. "Not exactly."

"What do you mean, not exactly?"

"She still wants me to have that threeway."

"Just tell her no. She can't force you to do anything you don't want to do."

"I know but it's a bit more complicated than that."

"Complicated how?"

A small smile played on his lips. "She said that if I fulfil her fantasy then she will fulfil one of mine."

"That's not complicated, Gavin, that's desperate."

"Call it what you like but it's an offer I find very tempting."

"Great," I huffed. "So your dick did all the thinking."

"Not all of it. My heart too." He looked at me almost pleadingly. "I really like her, Mikey. Maybe more than like."

Uh oh...

"But surely you don't like her enough to bone another dude." I feigned disgust at the thought of two men fucking. "That's not who you are."

"Fiona knows that but she also said that just because I'm not gay doesn't mean I can't be adventurous. And maybe she's right. I've never been scared to try new shit in the past. I ate snails at a French restaurant once."

"There's a difference between trying foreign cuisine and taking a cock up your ass."

"Whoa, whoa. Let's not get ahead of ourselves." He laughed like it was a joke, although he did look uncomfortable. "I haven't actually agreed to do anything yet. Just told her I would *consider* it. Under normal circumstances I would have told her to forget it but she has promised to fulfil my fantasy in return."

"Sometimes fantasies should just stay fantasies," I said, sounding more like the parental figure.

"You're probably right," he started, leaning back a little on his chair, "but it's fun to imagine what it would be like to turn a fantasy into a reality. I'd rather not tell her no to the threeway just yet so I can at least pretend for a little longer that my fantasy is coming true."

"I guess that makes sense," I said. "But what happens when you eventually tell her no?"

Gavin shrugged. "I guess we will cross that bridge when we come to it."

I got lost in a day dream of Fiona having a hissy fit and throwing him out of her house when he finally broke the news to her that he wouldn't be giving her what she wanted.

Gavin's voice cut through my reverie. "Are you going to ask me what it is?"

"Ask you what what is?"

"My fantasy." He looked at me. Not blushing, not even a little embarrassed. "It's something I've always wanted to do. I asked your mother a few times but she always said no."

"TMI."

"Sorry." He snicker-snorted. "I probably should keep it to myself."

"Nar, tell me. What's the fantasy?"

"Well..." he paused as if awaiting an imaginary drumroll. "It's to sit down with beer and pizza and watch the first three Die-Hard movies in one night."

"That's it?" How boring was this man? "You must be able to find a Bruce Willis fan somewhere."

"But I'd have a buddy with me and the girl would suck both our cocks through the whole thing. Then we'd take turns fucking her after the movies all finished."

"Fucking hell. That'd take like six hours or more. She'd end up with lockjaw."

"Hence it is a fantasy," he replied wistfully. "And as hot as it would be I just don't know if I can give Fiona what she wants."

Although he sounded more than a little disappointed at the thought of missing out on his Die-Hard suckathon, I was relieved to hear him sounding more realistic. Gavin couldn't give Fiona what she wanted. He knew that. I knew that. And so would Fiona if she wasn't such a crazy and demanding bitch. While I hated to think of Gavin being hurt when they eventually would break up—no doubt after he told Fiona no to the threeway—I knew it was for the best. She wasn't right for him.

I asked, "In this fantasy of yours who's the buddy you invite?"

"Trent, of course."

"Trent?" I squawked.

"Yeah. He's my best mate. It's one of his fantasies too. We made a pact as teenagers that if either of us ever got a chick willing to do it we'd invite the other over."

I laughed. "Fiona will have to try and find his cock under his rolls of fat first."

"He's not that fat."

"He's not that thin either."

"True that," Gavin agreed. "But he wasn't such a lard ass back when we were kids. He was actually a really handsome dude once upon a time."

"Saggy gut issues aside, there is also the slight problem that he's married."

"I don't think that would be a problem. You've seen Donna. Any man would be gagging for a nibble on a different plate after porking that thing for fifteen years."

"That's my adventurous saddo daddy. Chauvinistic as always."

Gavin chuckled as he glanced up at the clock. "Well, this saddo daddy better get his ass to work if he doesn't want to be late. Did you want me to leave you money for dinner or will you be a big boy and fend for yourself?"

"I think I'll be a big boy and fend for myself."

"Cool, cool. Catch ya later, bucko."

After Gavin left, I returned to my bedroom to see if Jockey had replied to my message. Judging by the flashing blue light coming from my phone it looked like he had. With a smile on my face, I checked the message to see Jockey's excited response.

My eyes widened at what he'd sent back. "What the shitting fuck?"

Jockey: Thanks for the apology but you know the answer.

I don't actually, that's why I was asking, dipshit. I knew better than to respond with that so I simplified my response to something less insulting.

Michael: Is that a yes or a no?

Jockey: No.

"What do you mean no?" I stared at the screen, unable to believe his audacity to turn down what I considered a generous and fair offer.

Michael: Why not?

Jockey: I don't suck beta dick. The only way I'd even consider sucking your dick again is if you agree to become my faggot.

Michael: I'm not a faggot!

Jockey. Not officially. But you could be mine if you wanted. The offer still stands.

Michael: That's never happening. So I suggest you drop it.

Jockey. OK.

That casual don't-give-a-fuck response got under my skin. How fucking dare he be so cool with me telling him he couldn't fuck me again. He was supposed to text back pleading with me to change my mind.

Ten minutes went by and my sour mood got the better of me. I picked up my phone again.

Michael: Why are you being such a dick?

Jockey: What have I been a dick about?

Michael: This whole faggot shit. I don't want Friday nights just to be me getting bummed. That's not fair.

Jockey: Life's not fair.

I didn't know what to say to that other than 'fuck you' but as I was about to type that, another message came through.

Jockey: And there's way more to being a faggot than just being bummed.

This was when I should have finished the 'fuck you' but curiosity got the better of me.

Michael: Like what?

I could see he was typing back but it took ages. He stopped and started, as if changing his mind, then after two minutes the message finally arrived.

Jockey: If a faggot wants to know what is required of it the first thing the faggot has to do is admit to itself it's a faggot. Then it would put on yellow briefs and go confess the same thing to its alpha (in person) while also telling its alpha why it wants that alpha to own its pussy.

I was too taken aback by how nutty it sounded to be offended.

Michael: Yellow briefs?

Jockey: Yes. The faggot must wear Yellow briefs. Very important.

Michael: Why is that important?

Jockey: If you were an alpha male or an owned faggot then you would know.

Michael: Don't be a dick.

He didn't respond. But I wasn't about to be outsmarted by a guy who thought Uzbekistan was a flavour of mayonnaise. So I searched the internet to find the answer, keen to text him back like the little know-it-all I was often accused of being. Unfortunately the search returned nothing other than far too many images of grey-haired men in yellow spandex.

Michael: You're making the yellow briefs thing up.

Jockey: And you're asking questions you don't have the right to know the answers to. Unless...

Michael: In your dreams freak. Just tell me what it means.

Jockey: If you want to know so badly then you know what to do.

Another message came through from him.

Jockey: Got to get back to work now. Talk later xx

“You can shove those kisses right up your lanky ass,” I cursed at my phone, damn near ready to hurl the bloody thing across the room. Calming myself down, I then went through and deleted the message history. I wasn’t letting the prick violate my inbox with his kinky bullshit.

Yellow briefs? What the actual fuck?

For starters, it made no fucking sense. Why would he expect someone to turn up to his house wearing yellow undies? And second, who the fuck owns a pair of yellow undies? I sure as shit didn’t. Not that it mattered because it would be a cold day in hell before I turned up there in a pair of yellow underwear.

Chapter 10

STARTING AT ELEVEN meant my day had been varied. I had started off in the kitchen working alongside Julie the chef before working on the counter after the day staff left at four. This is when business dried up and the café morphed into bar mode. It was also when the pair working the closing shift came in. Today it was Chad and the newest employee, a Canadian backpacker called Jason. The little I had worked with Jason was enough to know the guy was uber woke, and I was already cringing at the thought of Jason working with *the Chadster*.

My boss's tactic of rostering her pussy-mad son on to only work with other men had not gone unnoticed by Chad. As soon as he'd walked in the door he began complaining to me and Jason about being stuck in "a sausage fest" and that he knew what his mother was up to. "No offence boys but I'd rather be working with the girls. Especially that Vicky. I ain't sampled her tiny titties yet."

The more Chad spoke the more I expected Jason to go nuclear with allegations of bigotry while performing a dance of wounded feelings to the sound of Gay Whale songs and finger clicking fair-trade instruments made by indigenous children. While that did not eventuate, I could tell Jason was on the verge of biting off his own tongue.

I'd worked enough closing shifts with Chad by this stage that I'd finally climatised to his big personality. The guy may have been a fake hipster, and a bit of an idiot, but I'd decided he was mostly harmless. So while Jason suppressed his outrage at our boss's son's hyper-sexual spiels, I found myself smiling and even laughing occasionally. Especially when Chad recounted a story about losing his virginity at fourteen to a substitute teacher called Miss Wilkins. The story was clearly made up but I sort of appreciated the effort he'd gone to in a bid to make it seem believable and entertaining.

I think I was also more receptive to his stories because I was desperate to be taken out of my own thoughts that continued to circle back to what had happened at Hickford Park. No matter how many times I'd brushed my teeth in the last 48 hours, I couldn't get the taste of Rowan Quayle's dick out of my mouth. I also couldn't forget how he'd admitted to sniffing Brian's shoes and rubbing his balls on his pillows. It was downright horrifying. Did Brian have any idea? I doubted it. Brian had always considered his father his hero, constantly telling anyone who would listen how he hoped to grow up to be just like him.

You might want to re-evaluate that goal, mate.

As soon as the clock struck six o'clock, I undid the manbun I was forced to wear my hair in during café hours then told Chad my shift was over and made my way towards the door. Free at last, I wasn't going to spend a minute longer at work than I needed to. Chad called after me, but I pretended that I hadn't heard. He hadn't been as painful to work with today but that didn't mean I wanted to hang around and talk while not being paid.

The walk home usually took me half an hour, but I decided to stop off at the new Kmart that had opened last week. I hadn't been yet and was keen to scope out all the cheap shit on offer.

Anyone not from a small town probably doesn't realise how much of a big deal something like Kmart opening up is. For backwater shitholes like Moa Hill it's our version of the King's coronation. Ever since plans to open the store were made public a year ago, the local newspaper had been running stories most weeks about all the "Exciting growth" and "Future developments" our town could expect in coming years. Personally, I wasn't convinced, at least not until Wendy's or Carl's Jr came to town.

As predicted, Kmart was packed, still riding on the buzz of being newly opened. Wandering through the aisles I bumped into several familiar faces; my former history teacher Mr Wilde, two girls I used to work with at my last job and Gavin's best mate Trent.

Trent was a talker and could chew your ear off if you let him. And that's what was happening to me in the sporting goods aisle as Trent went on and fucking on about how he'd just joined his work's social club's cricket team.

At thirty-six, Trent was the same age as Gavin but he looked older. I wondered if it had something to do with having five kids under the age of seven. His shaggy brown hair was dusted with grey and thinning. He'd once had the body of an athlete, albeit a short one, but was now pot-bellied and pudgy in the face.

"Donna suggested I get back playing sport again. Said it would be a good way for me to lose a few pounds." Without meaning to my eyes dropped to his gut. "I figured it would be a good idea, especially after my last trip to the doctor where he warned me if I didn't start living a healthier lifestyle I'd wind up diabetic before I turned forty."

It was hard to believe that in his day Trent Pembroke had been one of the best-looking guys back in his hometown of Invercargill. You certainly couldn't tell by looking at him. Along with Gavin they'd been high school jocks who ploughed their way through all the pretty girls and—if their stories were to be believed—a couple of the pretty girls' mothers.

To be honest, I don't know how true some of their tales were but I had seen Gavin's yearbook and the pair of them certainly looked like they'd been popular with their rebel sneers and handsome faces. They looked like the sort of guys who'd never have been friends with a guy like me at school. Thankfully the nearly twenty years it had been since Gavin had been at high school meant he'd been clueless as to where I sat on my high school's popularity scale, and more often than not he just assumed I was every bit as cool as he'd once been. *Ha!*

Trent's voice nattered on. "I also thought it might set a good example to the kids to see their old man out there being active. Tyler's coming up eight now so I'm hoping if he sees me batting a ball about it might motivate him to try out for his school's cricket team."

"That sounds like a good idea," I replied, wondering when I could make a break for it.

"You ain't seen the kids for a while, have you?"

"Probably not since last Christmas."

"Wow. They've grown up so much." He reached into his pocket and fished out his phone.

Please not that. Please not that. Please not that.

"See. Here's Olivia. She's getting to be such a big girl."

Fuck... It's that.

Yep. I was cornered with an overly chatty proud father and I was now being inflicted with pictures of his little angels. *Somebody shoot me now.*

"I tell ya, having kids certainly keeps you on your toes. I've told Gavin he doesn't know what he's missing."

"Yeah."

"He says he happy with just one though."

I wondered who the *one* was until I realised it was me. That was weird. Gavin thinking of me as his son. But a good weird, I suppose.

Swiping to the next picture in his phone, Trent said, "But I've told him it's different when the your own. It means more."

That killed the good weird on the spot and Trent instantly realised what he'd said.

"Shit. I didn't mean it like that." He looked panicked. "It's just... um..."

"It's okay, Trent. I know Gavin's not my dad or anything like that. He's more like a..." I struggled to think of what to call him. With a shrug I said, "I don't know what he's like. Just Gavin, I guess."

"Yep." Trent smiled. "Just Gavin."

I could tell Trent was still feeling awkward from his previous comment and I hoped it would serve as my chance to escape. But just as I was about to tell him I had to get going his phone bleeped loudly in his hand.

"Speak of the devil." Trent swiped the screen and started reading the text which I assumed was from Gavin. "That sounds like fun."

"What's that?"

"Gavin just asked if I fancied catching up for a movie marathon next week." Face still aimed at his phone, Trent's pudgy fingers tapped back a response. "It's been years since I've watched those Die Hard films."

Chapter 11

AS I KNOCKED ON THE door to Jockey's sleepout I was nervous how he would react to me turning up uninvited. We hadn't exactly parted on good terms last Friday and our text conversation this morning hadn't gone much better.

When he opened the door, a fresh surge of adrenaline kicked hard in my gut. He was barefoot in a sleeveless tee and camo shorts, and I thought, *Oh Christ, red is absolutely your colour.*

"Hi," he said, smiling and rubbing his hand up and down his forearm. "Come in."

His laptop was open on the dining table, and there was a league match playing on the TV. "I'm not interrupting, am I?"

He picked up the remote and clicked the game off. "No, wasn't really watching. The Warriors are playing like shit. As usual."

It felt awkward already and I contemplated bolting. "Are we cool?"

He hesitated longer than I liked before finally smiling. "Of course, bro. We're always cool."

I stepped inside and we exchanged our usual bro-hug. After that it was as if nothing had happened last Friday: no mention of arguments, disagreements, and no talk of blowjobs. Just two mates hanging out in a sleepout in desperate need of an open window to let out the smell of the tenant's body odour.

This was the side of Jockey I liked. He didn't hold grudges.

I appreciated the normalcy he was allowing our friendship to resume. I wanted to hold onto it for as long as I could and forget the drama spinning in my head. Hearing what Gavin had text Trent had shook me in a way I hadn't expected. My stepfather had either had a sudden change of heart since breakfast or he'd lied to me. Either way I still felt let down. It made me realise how people can do stupid things for no good fucking reason other than to get laid. More importantly: was I one of those people?

"So what did you get up to today?" Jockey asked.

"Not much. Went to work. Stopped by Kmart for a look then went home to have some dinner before coming here."

"How was Kmart? I still ain't been to check it out yet."

"Really busy. Every man and his dog was there. It took me nearly thirty minutes waiting in line at the checkout."

"I can imagine."

Jockey began to talk about his day and gave me an update about the progress being made on his latest worksite. I nodded along in the right places, but I zoned out, not really knowing or caring what sort of plasterboard was being used to line a yet to be opened dental surgery in town.

I was tempted to tell him about Gavin and Fiona, and how she'd convinced Gavin to have sex with another guy. Ultimately I decided against it. Partly because I had yet to tell Jockey about the pair being together, but mostly because it was Gavin's private business. I couldn't imagine he'd be happy people finding out he was bending his sexuality in exchange for a silly fantasy deal he'd made with a mate in high school.

It bugged me to think Fiona had the power to make men go against their natural inclinations just to please her. Then I realised that in Jockey's case it hadn't been against his natural inclinations; the dude was more than partial to a bit of cock. But Gavin wasn't like that, and it just seemed fucked up that someone would try and make him something he wasn't.

I wondered if Gavin had already done the deed to earn his movie marathon fantasy. But that seemed unlikely. I doubted very much he would have a threesome at Fiona's house when her kids were home. He was a horny bastard like most men but he was a horny bastard with at least a few morals.

I suddenly snapped out of my brooding when I heard Jockey clicking his fingers and say, "Yoohoo. Earth to Mikey."

"Sorry." I shook my head. "What did you say?"

"I just said I've gotta head to bed soon. I'm fucking knackered and I've got an early start in the morning."

"You do?" My voice bubbled in panic.

"Yeah, I'm helping out on a worksite at the old hospital. Some out-of-towner is converting it into apartments. It's gonna be hard yakka so I'm gonna need my beauty sleep."

Jockey's impending bedtime jolted me. I suddenly felt like I was standing on the edge of a cliff with a crazed gunman at my back. My heart started racing and I could feel my palms getting sweaty.

"Are you alright, bro?" Jockey asked. "You look worried about something?"

"I'm fine." I fought my nerves and smiled. "I just remembered I forgot to tell you what I found at Kmart."

"What's that?"

Just do it. Just do it. Just do it.

With a heavy sigh, I got to my feet and lowered the front of my jeans to flash him what I had purchased.

Jockey's jaw twitched.

"What do you think?" I lowered my jeans even further, showing off the swell of my fabric-clad cock.

"They look nice." Licking his predator lips, Jockey's dark eyes scrutinized my bulge. "Boys like you suit yellow undies."

Embarrassed, I blushed and looked away. Was I making a mistake?

Jockey also seemed a little uneasy, but he was attempting to disguise it. With an overly casual yawn, he stretched his arms and turned his body so that he was facing me. He spread his legs wide and placed a hand on the crotch of his shorts, rubbing his cock through the material. His eyes gleamed when they met mine; he was looking up under his brows at me in a funny cocky way that made me suspect he knew things which I did not know and that he had some peculiar advantage over me for the knowledge.

I suppose he did. He had the answers to questions I needed answered.

The silence seemed to last forever, buzzing with unspoken sexual tension.

Then...

"Like I said, early start for me in the morning so I better hit the hay."

What was happening? I was wearing the yellow briefs like he'd asked. Had I done something wrong? Was it all a joke? I pulled my jeans back up, muttering a quiet apology for keeping him up so late.

"I guess I'll see you on Friday," Jockey said. "Unless of course there's something else you have to say to me."

The penny dropped. I still had one thing left to do.

"Now that you mention it," I said as I scratched my neck, "there is something I've been wanting to tell you."

"And what's that?"

"That I would—" I struggled to speak through the lump in my throat. "Sorry, man. This is way harder than I thought it would be."

"That's okay, dog. If you've got something important you need to get off your chest then I'm all ears."

I bit the inside of my cheek and nodded. "I just wanted you to know that I'm a faggot."

He sat there with his hands clasped together, nodding slowly. "I thought that might be what you wanted to tell me. Anything else?"

"And..." My ego was in genuine pain but I'd come too far now. "I was wondering if you'd be interested in owning my pussy."

"So you wanna be my faggot, aye? My personal property?"

"Yes."

"And why do you want me to own your pussy, Michael?"

The way he said my full name felt like sorcery, a spell being cast to further weaken my usual know-it-all confidence.

"What's the matter?" Jockey asked. "Cat got your tongue? Surely you must know why you want me to own your pussy?"

I'd rehearsed my response to this ever since I had bought the yellow briefs, but now all those words abandoned me. "I had a whole speech planned but I've forgotten it."

"Fuck the speech, just tell the truth. Tell me why *I'm* the right man for the job of taming your pussy. I respect honesty, Mike. I also expect it. Right now more than ever."

As I stood there nervously rubbing my heels together, I realised Jockey was right. The truth was all I had in this moment. So, after a deep breath followed by an equally deep exhale, I told Jockey Savage exactly why he was the right man for the job.

"As much as it pisses me off to admit this, I enjoyed being fucked by you. Like, *really* enjoyed it. I know it was my first time ever having sex but I could still tell that you're a great fuck. You just..." I lost my voice as a bashful smile broke out on my face. "I used to laugh to myself when you'd spout shit like '*I'm a real man*' and '*I'm an alpha male*', but now I know you weren't talking shit. You've got the moves to back it up, bro. And the cock! Talk about having a talented dick. And big! Definitely bigger than what I thought it was. To be honest, I'm actually sort of embarrassed you sucked me off for so long when I should have been the one on his knees. And if this is what I am. A faggot. Then I want someone I can trust to show me the way. Someone like you. And if I get my cock sucked in return then that's a bonus."

After a long beat of silence, Jockey replied, "I'm proud of you, Mikey. That took a lot of balls to say what you just did."

"Thank you."

"And I appreciate you acknowledging I have the superior dick. It's important for a faggot to know his cock is less worthy." He leaned back on his bed, tracing a fingertip over the bulge in his shorts. "But you do know that being my faggot doesn't guarantee you blowjobs, right? You'd have to earn them."

"I know. But I'm still keen to be your faggot." That fucking word still tasted like shit coming out of my mouth, but it was getting easier to say.

"It's a pretty big responsibility being an alpha male's faggot. It ain't an easy life, dog. You gotta work hard to please a real man. You gotta keep his belly full and his balls empty."

"I don't mind working hard."

"We'll see. Maybe."

"Maybe?"

"You don't know what the role entails yet. You can't sign up for something you know didley squat about."

"That's why I'm here. So you can tell me what to expect."

Jockey pointed to the floor in front of where I was standing. "Sit," he growled as if he were talking to a dog.

I did as I was told, watching as he got to his feet and walked over to the bookshelf on the wall behind me. He then came and stood in front of me and passed me an A4 white envelope.

"Everything you need to know about becoming my faggot is in here. But I don't want you opening it until you get home though. Understood?"

I nodded.

"If after reading it you're still keen to be owned by me then you will sign it and bring it back."

"Why can't I just sign it now?"

"Because right now you're horny as fuck and will sign anything put in front of you. That's not the right head space to be in to sign something like this. What you need to do is take it home, read it, then jerk off and read it again. Wank and repeat, wank and repeat."

"I'm guessing whatever is in the contract is pretty intense then."

"Of course it's intense. Inside that envelope is a contract where you're essentially giving another person, *me*, ownership of your body. This ain't no silly game, Mikey. This is the real deal. So I need you to take it very seriously."

I don't think I'd ever seen Jockey act and sound so serious before.

Glancing up at my superior, I asked, "How come you have something like this just laying around?"

"I wrote it especially for us. I've been working on it the past few days. I had a feeling we'd find ourselves in this situation."

"You did?"

"I could tell the night I fucked you that you've got a hungry cunt and would probably need a real man to feed it."

My cheeks roasted with a blush. "What happens if I don't sign it?"

"You'll still be a faggot. You've just admitted that's what you are. There's no taking that back. And because you are a faggot I'll treat you accordingly from now on."

"Meaning?"

"When you visit me in future I will expect you to sit on the floor like you are now. You only take a seat on the couch or my bed if I give you permission. And if at any time you don't like being made sit on the floor then you know where the door is." He reached down and gave his nuts a good scratch, the movement giving away that I wasn't the only one with a boner right now. "If we're out in public things will still be the same as they've always been, but the moment we're alone you will be reminded of your place. Which means I will call you a faggot to your face. You can't escape that. After all, you were the dumb bitch who let yourself get cornholed. Not me."

Jockey was on a power trip that he'd probably only ever fantasised about in his wildest wet dreams. Now here he was wielding a darkness that for years he'd had to keep locked up in the cesspit of his filthy mind. It made me hate him. It also made me want him to fuck me even more. So he was probably right about me being a dumb bitch.

Silence consumed the room once again as he glared down at me; his gaze cold and hard. Right now his eyes looked more like weapons than something he used to see with. It was unnerving, belittling, disarming. Up till now I felt like I'd kept my shit together pretty well, but the longer he stared at me without speaking I found myself at risk of unravelling.

Finally, he broke the quiet with a command. "Follow me."

Leaving the envelope on the floor, I followed him into the bathroom where he told me to strip my clothes off. He stuck his hand out to be passed each item until I was eventually standing before him without a stitch of clothing. He placed my clothes and shoes on a chair beside the bathtub then turned around and stared, gazing up and down my naked body.

The intense scrutiny of his unyielding gaze had me shivering with excitement, with fear. Then he reached out and took my cock in his hand. I closed my eyes and moaned, grateful for his touch, hoping he would stroke me to orgasm.

But he only squeezed it, as if he were testing the size and hardness. At the same time he squeezed his own erection through his shorts. Then he released me and took a step back.

Again he stared at me, rubbing his meat. I was afraid to touch myself with him watching. So I stood, painfully aware of my nakedness and the hardness of my cock, and waited for him to tell me what he wanted.

He dug a hand inside his pocket and pulled out his phone "I know you haven't signed the contract yet but do you mind if I take a picture of your dick?"

"Why do you want to take a picture of my dick?"

"Because I want to."

A bit rude perhaps, but I figured it was as good a reason as any. "Okay. If you want."

Kneeling in front of me, he zoomed in with the camera on his phone and took a series of close-up shots of my dick. *Click.*

Click. Click. He wrapped his fingers round my shaft, gave it a couple squeezes until I leaked a bead of pearly precum. *Click. Click.*

"Turn around so I can get some pics of your ass."

I did as he said, turning to face the bathroom mirror. What I saw looking back at me was a face of deep shame. I couldn't believe what I was allowing him to do; taking pictures of my naked body. In the back of my mind I knew it was foolish to allow another person to take those sorts of images, but something kept overriding the sensible part of my brain.

Click. Click. Click.

"Bend over and spread your cheeks. I want to get some of your pussy hole."

As I bent over, sacrificing another piece of dignity, I felt the tip of my cock jab against my belly. I avoided looking at it, embarrassed by its hardness.

"I still can't believe I've had my cock up there." His hot breath wafted over the tiny orifice. Then he probed the crack with his fingers and tugged at the short hairs, examining my asshole as if he had never looked at one before. "It still looks virginal. Tight as fuck. But a few weeks of regular fucking should change that."

Click. Click. Click. Click.

Then there was silence.

It lingered...

"Can I turn around now?" I asked.

"Not yet. I'll tell you when you can."

I soon heard the sound of water, a steady trickle and the echo of splashes. When the noise finally stopped, I heard Jockey clear his throat. "You can turn back around now," he said.

As soon as I did, I noticed that my clothes had been moved. He'd put them in the bath tub. They were wet. Saturated. "What did you do?"

"What do you think?"

At first I assumed he'd turned on the tap but as I stepped closer I could smell the undeniable stench of urine. "You pissed on my clothes?" My voice was screechy, panicky. "Why would you do something like that?"

He chuckled, a short, barking, contemptuous sound. "You text this morning asking to know the significance of yellow. I just showed you."

Slack-jawed, I continued to stare at my clothes bathing in puddles of piss.

"You can put them back on now," he said.

"What?"

"You heard me, faggot. Put on your pissy clothes."

Irritation crawled up my throat, like a cocktail of Smirnoff and old socks. I felt my hands curl into fists, rage bubbling up inside me. Jockey noticed and he shot me a look that dared me to punch him. But then my anger slowly receded and I unclenched my fists.

One by one, I slowly put my piss-soaked clothes back on. The wet material made me grimace as it warmed my skin before quickly cooling. The worst part was sitting down on the edge of the bath to put my shoes and socks on. He'd pissed inside each sneaker; enough piss in each to ensure that even if they were dried out they'd always have *his* smell.

Jockey stood there smirking like an asshole. It was clear how much he was enjoying this. "Don't look so grumpy. A faggot should be proud to have his man's juice on him. And judging my how much you fucking stink it's safe to say you're covered in it."

I scowled but remained silent.

"Now say 'thank you, Jockey, for pissing on my clothes.'"

I chewed my lip so hard it was almost bleeding. I counted ten heartbeats before I managed to open my mouth. Ten rapid, throbbing pulses like drumbeats across my forehead. I wanted to say, *Go to hell, asshole.*

Instead I repeated what needed to be said: "Thank you, Jockey, for pissing on my clothes."

"You're very welcome, Mike. Now go get the envelope and take your faggot ass home so I can get to bed."

He led me to the door to show me out. Just before I stepped outside, he stroked the side of my face and said, "Make sure you always remember tonight. It's the night you admitted you're a faggot. And there's no taking that back." He exhaled heavily, fanning my face with his terrifyingly sweet breath. "Even if you don't sign that contract we will both still know what you are. From now until the day you die you will be beneath me."

His words were harsh and icy but it was the look on his face that left me cold and shattered inside. He was no longer looking at me with the warmth of friendship, but with pure contempt, even arrogance, the way I imagined so many others in this town regarded him.

With the door closed behind me, I made my way into the night. The air outside was fresh and clean but it failed miserably in dislodging the smell clinging to my juicy clothes. A smell that was slowly soaking into my skin. Every step I took unleashed a squish of Jockey's piss between my toes, my shoes making bubbly noises when they hit the ground.

I realised this was about more than humiliation. Like some wild animal, Jockey had sprayed my clothes and marked me as his territory.

Which meant he was right.

I would always be beneath him now.

Chapter 12

WORK THE NEXT DAY WAS like walking in thick winter fog; cold and disorientating. Accompanying my feeling of being lost was a sense of being dirty and unclean. I'd had two showers since walking home last night in clothes drenched with jockey's piss but I still felt like I had urine soaked into my skin. I began to wonder if I'd ever feel clean again.

Thankfully Gavin had still been out when I had returned home with soggy footsteps. It was just as well because I don't know if he would have bought the story I was going to tell him about how some random car driving past had hurled water balloons filled with piss at me out their window. After stripping out of my urinated clothes, I'd sat in the shower until the water ran cold. I'd been numb. I was still numb. Unable to believe how I'd allowed a dumb curiosity to lead me to Jockey's doorstep. Even if it was more than mere curiosity that had lured me to Jockey's sleepout, I hadn't gone there expecting to be sent home stinking like a urinal cake. It was so fucking disrespectful. So not the way I was used to being treated.

When the bar's sole customer left, I went out back to fetch a box of Smirnoff that were running low in the bar fridge. I knelt down to restock the shelf, catching my reflection on the glass door of the fridge. The way it resembled a framed snapshot made me grimace as I recalled the naked pictures Jockey had taken of me.

What the fuck was I thinking?

I just hoped Jockey would delete them when I asked him to. Or at the very least promise to never show anyone. The only way I could think to fix things was to tell him last night had all been a joke, nothing serious. But I knew in my heart that wasn't going to work. The hard look in his eyes, the cruel tone of his voice...it had all been so permanent. He would never view me as Michael Freeman the regular guy anymore. He would always consider me a—

"Michael!"

I popped up from behind the bar to find Brian's mother standing the other side of the bar. My initial assumption was she'd found out about what I'd done with her husband and she'd come in to give me a slap. But when I saw her smile I realised my imagination, and guilt, was running away on me. Just coming in the door was her scumbag husband who did not look pleased to be here; clearly dragged in by his wife. He had a deer-in-the-headlights expression when he locked eyes on me, but he masked it faster than I did.

"Are you okay?" Mrs Quayle asked me. "You look like you've seen a ghost?"

"Sorry. I'm just feeling a bit tired." I forced myself to smile. "It's been a long shift."

"Just think of the money," she said in a perky tone. "That's what I always say."

With a clenched jaw, Mr Quayle sat down beside his wife. "Good evening, Michael."

"Good evening."

"Rowan and I are about to go to the movies," Mrs Quayle said, oblivious to the fact her husband's cock had been in my mouth three days ago. "It's been ages since we've seen a film on the big screen so I thought it was high time he took me out for dinner and a movie."

Mr Quayle shot another glance at me, and there was no mistaking his discomfort. I could almost see it in his eyes; the silent chant of *please don't say anything inappropriate, please don't ruin my marriage, please just shut the hell up.*

Lowering her voice to a hushed whisper, Mrs Quayle said, "You know how I just asked you if you'd seen a ghost?"

"Yeah?"

"I worked in a bar once when I was a law student in Auckland and it was haunted." She tapped her husband's arm. "Do you remember, Rowan?"

"I do, darling." Mr Quayle tried to smile, but his mouth crumbled under the effort. "It was in the old art gallery, was it not?"

"Yes." She leaned closer to me. "Talk about spooky."

While Mrs Quayle reiterated the story about her haunted workplace, I could feel Mr Quayle eyeballing me. I couldn't tell if it was anger or lingering fear. But his eyes were on me, soaking me in. I found myself doing the same to him whenever his wife wasn't looking, taking a good look at the baby boomer who'd confessed to sniffing his own son's sneakers.

He looked so much like Brian—bookishly handsome—but had sixty years' worth of creases, lines and wrinkles framed by greying brown hair and blue eyes that had less spark than his son. He was dressed in a short-sleeve button-down, untucked for a jaunty presentation, thin arms on display. Tan chinos and brown loafers finished the ensemble. He wasn't about to walk the runway at London fashion week but it was far trendier than what he'd usually wear—indicating his wife had most likely picked the outfit for him.

At least he isn't liver spot old, I told myself. *And he's not fat. If anything he is probably considered super fit for a guy his age.*

Regardless of those points I still couldn't fight the tummy-wobbling shame that I'd sucked a cock that had been on this earth for sixty years. Add to that the guilt from knowing I'd helped the man commit adultery and I was wishing I was anywhere else than right here right now.

Mrs Quayle's story was interrupted by her cell phone ringing. When she pulled it out of her handbag, she released a loud sigh and declared. "I better take this." She looked at her husband and added, "It's that client I was telling you about."

"Hello," she said and proceeded to make her way outside.

Don't go! Come back!

While my anxiety skyrocketed, Mr Quayle's all but vanished. Where there had been unease I could now see unspoken desire. I just prayed that whatever he was thinking remained unspoken.

That prayer was not answered.

"Your dick tasted delicious, Michael." He met my gaze and grinned, a slick and slimy spreading of his lips. "One of the yummiest I have ever had the privilege of sucking."

I was sure that my entire face was flushed with heat, but I tried to remain composed. "Mr Quayle, I—"

"Please, call me Rowan. I think after what happened the other day we deserve to be on a first name basis."

"Rowan..." His name was all that would come out.

"I always knew you would have a beautiful dick but I never knew it would taste so good."

"Thank you." My gratitude came out by accident and almost sounded flirty. It wasn't my intention.

"Did you like my cock?" he asked softly. "It's a good size, isn't it? Quite the mouthful I've been told."

There was no fucking way I was going to answer that question.

"You won't tell Brian about the things I said?" his voice remained hushed, secretive. "Because I didn't mean them. I was just talking nonsense."

It was then I finally found my voice, triggered by his blatant lie.

"No you weren't," I snapped. "You meant every word you said."

Rather than be annoyed by my frosty tone, he just smiled. "I suppose I did."

"So you admit it then?"

"Can you blame me? Brian is a very handsome young man."

"But he's your son!"

"I have never done anything untoward with Brian if that is what you are thinking. All I have ever done is admire from afar. Just like I have with you on occasion. But had I known you were like me then I might have made a move sooner."

"I'm nothing like you."

"Yes you are. We are both slaves to our desire, letting it take us to dark places for fulfilment."

"I was only at the park to use the toilet."

He regarded me with suspicion, and rightly so.

"Okay," I said. "I might have been there because I was curious but I honestly did not intend to hook up. And certainly not with you. You tricked me."

"I suppose I did." He sounded pleased with himself. "But it was worth it."

"Not for me."

"I know at your age I must seem terribly old, and perhaps I am, but as you can now testify a man's cock doesn't tend to wrinkle or sag with age. Provided they can get it up. And I most certainly can."

"I-I don't know what to say."

"You can say you'll be at the park next Tuesday. I'll be there until ten o'clock."

"I'm not going to the park ever again."

"Are you sure? I know a quiet spot there where no one will disturb us."

"I'm not interested in going to the pig pen, thanks." I hoped sharing that would make him think I wasn't as clueless as I actually was.

"You know about the pig pen?" He looked amused. "Have you partaken in the delightful events that go on there?"

"No. A friend told me about it."

"Does this friend have a name?"

"You won't know him."

"I might. I'm on quite good terms with most regulars there."

"Just how often do you bloody go there?"

"That's personal."

"Aren't you worried about being known as a Hickford Homo? There was that person taking pictures and putting them on the internet. If you get caught that would ruin your reputation for good. And possibly Mrs Quayle's."

"Oh, that just adds to the thrill," he said dryly. "Besides, that lowlife hasn't been there for ages."

It went quiet. Awkwardly so.

"Tell me, Michael. Are you a top or a bottom?"

"Now who's the one asking personal questions."

"Fair point." He exhaled slowly. "I go to the park three nights a week."

"Three nights a week?"

"I don't have sex every time I go there. Most of the time I just watch what goes on. Now your turn. Top or bottom?"

"I don't know," I said honestly. "I'm sort of new to this."

"I would have said you were a top a week ago but now I'm leaning towards you being a twinky bottom. I imagine you make the prettiest noises when you get buggered. I'd love the chance to get to hear them one day."

"That's not happening, Rowan. And if it's okay with you I'd rather we just pretend the other day never happened either. This is just too weird."

"I think that would be a shame, Michael. I have been thinking about you non-stop since our little dance in the loos."

"Yeah well... I've not been thinking about you."

"I doubt that. I know for a fact I would have been on your mind quite a bit. I'm your best friend's father and you sucked me off. Very well too." There was something sadistic about his tone, like he was weaponizing the experience against me. "And I'm very serious about wanting to meet up again. It doesn't have to be at the park. I could get us a hotel room for the night. Take you out for dinner. Then we could go back to the room and enjoy ourselves properly."

"No thank you."

"I would make it worth your while."

"Taking me out for a meal is not making it worth my while."

He laughed like I was an idiot. "I'm not talking about dinner, dear boy. I am talking about paying you money. I'm a very wealthy man and I can reward pretty young things like yourself very handsomely if they do what I say."

Brian's father was giving me the creeps in a big way. This wasn't the sheepish and conservative family man I knew—a man who'd always struck me as being easily embarrassed. This guy right now didn't seem like he was capable of embarrassment.

"You can't buy me."

"I'm not *buying* you, Michael. I'd be hiring your services. It would be very respectful, and generous."

"Generous? Ha! I've seen what you pay to *hire* a young guy's services. You paid that blond boy peanuts."

"That's because he was only worth peanuts." He looked at me sharply. "Boys like that are trash and you don't pay top dollar for trash. But you're not trash. You are top shelf quality and therefore I am willing to pay a top shelf price."

I was tempted to ask him how much but my moral compass was too strong. "I'm not a prostitute."

"Everybody has a price," he said coldly. "Even young men with too much pride for their own good."

It almost sounded like a threat and I didn't appreciate it. After what had happened with Jockey I was not about to let another man view me as some sort of sex object.

"Well, I must be the exception to the rule," I said, "because I don't have a price and I never will. So I'd appreciate it if you would kindly fuck off before I tell your wife about your little cocksucking hobby."

"There's no need to be rude, Michael."

"I think you'll find there is."

He laughed, unperturbed, and pulled something out of his wallet. "I want you to take this." He handed me what appeared to be his business card. "My work mobile is on there. If you change your mind and find yourself interested in discussing a deal then text me and let me know."

As soon as he left, I ripped the card in half and tossed it in the bin.

Chapter 13

***IF YOU ARE READING** this then that means you have admitted you're a faggot. Congratulations Michael Freeman. You should be proud of yourself for realising your place in the world and acknowledging your inferiority to real men such as myself.*

The intro to the five-page contract was infuriating to say the least. I imagined Jockey sitting at his laptop late into the night, typing away wearing nothing but a smile and a hard-on. I'd read the contract once when I got home last night, twice before going to work this morning, and now having just returned home from my shift this would be my fourth time reading it. I'd taken Jockey's advice about jerking off before reading it, hence five minutes earlier I'd flushed a wad of cum-stained loo paper down the toilet. It was good advice because it allowed me to read it with a clear head and see just how fucking insane the contract was.

Although I had no intention of signing it, I'd be lying if I said I didn't find its contents fascinating. It was more than just a contract; it also provided a window into Jockey's mind, and what I was seeing was dark and depraved. This was all the stuff I'd been curious to know when I'd turned up at Jockey's last night, keen for answers about something that seemed mysterious in sinful ways. I just wish he'd allowed me to read the document before my horny ass had bought the underwear and told him I was a faggot. But I could see why he hadn't let me read it sooner. This contract contained way too much personal information about him and his kinks to let me read it without having some sort of leverage over me. Which probably also explained why he'd taken pictures of my dick and asshole. I knew that if I whispered a word of what was in this contract to anyone then those pictures would make their way online. He hadn't said that but I could feel it in my bones. I'd given him a weapon he could use against me.

"Why did I have to be such a fucking idiot?" I muttered angrily to myself.

The simple answer to that was I'd been horny. So bloody horny.

The click of the kettle boiling let me know it was time to make myself a coffee. I lay the contract down on the table and went to the bench. As I poured the hot water into my mug, I wondered if I'd be better of having an ice tea instead. It was nearly eight p.m. but it was still balmy day outside. The weather hadn't been able to make up its mind if it wanted to rain or be sunny, creating one of those wet, sticky days that felt like you were walking under water. As I returned to the kitchen table with my cup of coffee, I glanced out the window at the empty carport and wondered when Gavin would be getting home.

I wonder if he's busy giving slutface what she wanted?

The thought had occurred to me several times throughout the day when I was able to stop myself thinking about Jockey's contract. Even if Gavin was desperate, desperate enough to bend his sexuality in exchange for some fantasy he and Trent had conjured up as dumb teenagers, then I couldn't imagine Gavin doing the threeway last night while Fiona's kids were under the same roof.

But something must have been agreed upon for Trent to have received that text.

I reminded myself it was none of my business. Besides, it wasn't like I could judge Gavin for thinking with his cock when my own dick had led me to an even more troubling situation. At least in Gavin's case it was a one-off event. He only had to do it once, get what he wanted, then move on. That wasn't the case for me. Even without signing the contract I knew I had done permanent damage by visiting Jockey last night in yellow underwear. I don't know what I thought would happen by going there and making such a twisted confession, but not for one minute did I expect to walk home covered in Jockey's piss. The most tragic part was how I had left there angry at him for not fucking me. I had been so horny last night I wouldn't have given a shit how he fucked me. There was no denying that I'd gone there wanting it. Wanting his dick. A part of me still did. But being okay with getting buggered, even regularly, was not the same thing as wanting to give another man ownership of your body.

It wasn't until I'd got home and had a wank in the shower that the reality of what had transpired between us really hit me. And it hit me so hard I'd collapsed against the tiles and slid to the floor, sitting there numb until the water had turned cold. I had just told my friend I was a faggot, and not just in the gay sense. I had admitted I was beneath him. Shit, I'd even got off on doing it. That's what confused me. How the fuck could I be turned on by something that left me feeling so cheap and disgusted with myself. The worst part was there was no taking back what I'd said. Jockey wouldn't let me. I had no doubt that the next time I visited him he would indeed make me sit my sorry ass on the floor. Jockey's outlook on sex and the hierarchy of men was bonkers, but a small part of my brain also understood how it made sense, which was crazy considering some of the wacky shit contained in the contract.

As my faggot your purpose and main priority will be my pleasure. You will need to become familiar with the things I like and do the upmost to please me. This includes how you present yourself. If I do not like what you are wearing then you will get changed into an outfit of my choosing.

You will never waste my seed. That means all cum must be taken either in your mouth or pussy. A faggot should always be focused on an Alpha's cock's pleasure, and cum is the result of that pleasure, and contains the Alpha's power.

You will be trained to view your pussy as your main sex organ. That means under no circumstances are you allowed to play with your dick without my permission. You must learn to gain sexual pleasure from your pussy. I have ways to help you with this.

Mondays will be known as milking day. If you fail to produce the amount of come I desire then you will be milked the following day. This is why it is important you do not masturbate without my permission. If I find out you are then I will have no choice but to lock your cock in chastity.

Some faggots find piss unappealing. Who cares? Piss comes from an Alpha's cock, so therefore it should be treated with respect. A faggot should learn to love and crave Alpha piss. And yes, this includes drinking it.

My stomach clenched as I imagined being forced to drink Jockey's piss. That wasn't the only clause in the contract that made me gag. There were plenty of others that left me nauseous and wondering how on earth he thought I would ever entertain such an arrangement. Some of it was downright laughable, like the part that said I would have to choose between getting a tattoo with Jockey's name or allow him to video me getting fucked at Hickford Park and then put it online.

But I wasn't laughing.

Maybe it was because I could imagine Jockey pulling off the role of alpha male. While most people in town considered him just a dopey stoner incapable of exerting power and control, I had firsthand experience of his dominance. Dude could fuck. Dude could fuck real well. Add to that his height and sizable dick it wasn't a stretch of the imagination to see him owning a faggot stupid enough to go along with these demands.

I turned the page and got to the section asking for my personal details: age, height, weight, shoe size, dick size etc. There were two columns, one for me to put my answers and another under the heading *At Inspection.* I had no idea what that meant but there was a small note at the bottom explaining that column was for him to fill out. There was even a section asking me about masturbation: how old was I when I started, how often I did it, and my technique.

Thirteen. Once or twice a day on average. Three fingers and a thumb wrapped around the shaft while tugging. But sometimes I just like to fuck my mattress or a pillow.

My mind may have gladly answered such questions but there was no way I would ever write that sort of shit down on paper. No one had the right to know those things. They were my secrets and mine alone.

However, buried amongst the invasive questions and outrageous sexual demands was a softer side that revealed how much Jockey valued honesty and loyalty. I guess I already knew that about him but the contract just reinforced those traits of his. And to be fair, the terms weren't *all* bad. In some ways I could he see how he might consider it fair and reasonable. For example, he was willing to pay for any expenses I might require like sex toys, personal grooming, health checkups and douching equipment. There was even an option for me to tick if I wanted to be taken out for dinner once a week.

As a responsible property owner I will ensure to maintain my asset (you the faggot) to make sure it continues giving me value in return. In the event of loaning my asset out to a friend (similar to how one may lend their car) they will be expected to treat the asset with the same care as I would.

I finally let out a chuckle at how business-minded he sounded. It was sort of cute, like a child playing grownups with their barbies or GI Joes—but with the total violation of human rights and bum sex thrown in. Still, what he was saying here made perfect sense. If Jockey wanted something as crazy as this to work then he would have his own set of responsibilities to make sure his faggot was taken care of. By the time I got to the last page where it asked for my signature, I almost felt sorry for him. He had put a lot of effort into writing this and in a weird way I felt flattered he'd gone to such trouble just for me. It seemed a shame it was all a waste of time but I could not give Jockey what he wanted. Despite telling him I was a faggot I still had too much self-respect to sign something like this, and not to mention a personality that meant I was allergic to being told what to do.

But there was still going to be the issue of how he'd treat me when we were alone, calling me a faggot to my face and being forced to sit on the floor. I figured the answer to that would be we hang out in town more often. Provided he kept the name-calling to a minimum I could probably live with it. Then the moment I found a new group of friends I could begin to distance myself from Jockey and the whole sadistic nightmare.

What about the sex?

I couldn't tell if that was me or my dick talking, but it was a good point. Before Jockey's cock had breached my asshole I had never imagined I could go that far with a guy, and enjoy it. Not only had I enjoyed being fucked, but I'd been amazed to discover I was attracted to the guy who was fucking me. Even though he'd been sucking me off for nearly two years, I'd never really viewed Jockey as sexually desirable before that night. He'd just been a mouth to nut into. Well, not anymore. I had now learned that beneath his army getup, tall slinky frame, and cocky demeanor, a storm of mayhem, danger, and sex swirled out of control.

Jockey wasn't classically handsome, which is probably why I'd failed to ever see his appeal before now. On some angles his face looked a bit ratty, his features a bit too sharp. He also lacked that blokey charm so many Kiwi women went for: the more rugged masculinity that men like Gavin and Trent had. Jockey's masculinity presented itself in a different way, more misfit than machismo. More thug than hero. More dirtbag than leading man. But despite all this I could now see what Fiona must have seen in him—a young man in his prime whose sexuality was dark, dangerous and addictive, and with a cock that had been engineered to claim and conquer.

It wouldn't be easy to switch off my lust for him but I would have to do exactly that if I wanted to avoid any further descent into depravity. Besides, he wasn't the only guy in town that would know how to fuck. Maybe I could look online or download an ap to find a guy keen to fool around. Ideally a guy who would let me fuck them too, since I was still pretty sure that was my preference. Cos if I were being honest, I would be signing that contract in a heartbeat if it meant I was the one being given ownership of Jockey's body.

Imagine it...

I went from flaccid to semihard as I pictured Jockey with his ankles behind his ears and me pounding the shit out of his virgin asshole. Dropping a hand between my legs, I squeezed my dick, encouraging its growth. Just as I was about to unzip my pants and rub one out right there in the kitchen, the sound of a vehicle coming down the drive had me glancing out the window.

Gavin was home.

I quickly rushed the contract into my bedroom and hid it in the drawer with Jockey's briefs. Then, after patting my crotch down to make sure I wasn't tenting, I returned to the kitchen and waited for Gavin to come inside. We hadn't spoken since yesterday and I was glad to see him. His friendly brown eyes and stubbled face was a welcome sight and provided some much-needed normality that had felt missing in my life these past 24 hours.

Gavin was whistling a happy tune to himself as he came inside. He greeted me with a friendly "Hey, Mikey" before telling me he was busting to take a piss. I stayed seated and waited for him to come back and tell me about his day. This was part of our routine. It didn't matter how dull and repetitive our lives were we always asked how each other's day was.

When he returned from the toilet, he fetched a beer from the fridge, cracking it open with a fierce glare on his face. I wondered what had happened in the space of two minutes to make him go from whistling happily to having a face like a cat's asshole. When he came to sit down at the table with me I saw what had him looking so disgruntled. He had piss stains down the front of his pale pants. Anyone would have thought he'd visited Jockey wearing yellow underwear.

"Fucking hell," I laughed, gaze aimed at his crotch. "Did you get any of it in the bowl?"

"I had a bit of a whoopsie." He smiled shyly, but refused to make eye contact. "Don't worry, I wiped up the mess."

"Were you pissing with your eyes shut or something?"

He blinked slowly, like a cat, then spoke.

"Nar. It's because of what I have on. Fiona told me I'd be better to sit down but I didn't listen."

"What do you have on?"

"Something Fiona gave to me." His voice was flat.

"What did she give you? Aside from chlamydia, that is."

He glowered. "That's not funny, Michael."

I was taken aback by his stern response. Gavin never snapped at me. "It was just a joke, man. Sheesh. Calm your farm."

His anger quickly receded and was replaced with a small smile. "Sorry, buddy. It's been a long day."

"No worries. So what did Fiona give you that's made you suddenly incontinent?"

"What we talk about stays between us. You know that, right?"

"I know that."

"Good, because the last thing I need is the guys at work hearing about this. They'd give me shit for weeks." He stared to make sure I understood before continuing. "Fiona gave me an early birthday present. A chastity device."

"A chastity device?"

My gaze drifted to Gavin's crotch, trying to see any telltale sign of the contraption.

"You know...something that goes over your cock so you can't play with yourself."

Little did Gavin realise but I knew very well what a chastity device was. I'd suffered through five days of wearing Jockey's old one to help give him a birthday to remember.

"Fiona made me put it on this morning and I gotta say I ain't loving it." His hand dipped to adjust himself. "If I had the key I'd take the bloody thing off right now but of course Fiona is keeping the key at her place for safe keeping."

"I don't suppose this has anything to do with you inviting Trent over for a movie marathon next week?"

Gavin flinched. "How do you know about that?"

"I was with him at Kmart when he got the text. I'm assuming this means you gave Fiona what she wanted." My tone was bitter. Resentful even. "I thought you said you weren't gonna do it. That's what you told me."

"I don't need your permission, Mike. I make my own decisions. You need to respect that."

"I know but... why'd you lie to me?"

His brows drew together and he stared down at his beer instead of looking at me. "Because you looked so disappointed with me when I began to talk about it. I'm having a hard enough time wrapping my brain around this threeway as it is without feeling like I'm letting you down." He finally looked back up and met my gaze. "While I don't need your permission, I do like to know I have your approval. Knowing that I didn't have that, I just told you what you wanted to hear."

I blinked down to my half-drank cup of coffee in front of me, turned it in little circles on the coaster. "I'm sorry if I made you feel bad. That wasn't my intention."

"I know. But hey, I guess I can tell you now that your ass needs to be out of the house Friday next week."

"So it hasn't happened yet?"

"Nope. That's why I've got this cunting thing on." His hand reached down to tug at the crotch of his pants again. "Fiona thought that if I wore this for the next few days it would help me put in a better performance. I guess it makes sense in a weird way. If I go a week without nutting then come next weekend I'll be so desperate to come I'll stick it in any hole. Even if it is attached to a pair of nuts."

"So you're, uh, going all the way?"

"It looks a lot like it." He took a swig on his beer. "I wasn't going to, but eventually I just though fuck it, why not. As Fiona said, it doesn't mean I'm queer or nuffin. Just adventurous."

"If you want to be adventurous then just go bungy jumping."

"That's what I said, but Fiona insists this will be more fun."

My stomach dropped into an abyss, and although I knew my irritation with Gavin's stupidity was wildly hypocritical, I couldn't rein it in. "I hope you know what you're getting yourself into."

Gavin laughed and rolled his eyes.

"What's so funny?" I demanded.

"You. You're such a worry wart."

"No I'm not."

"You are, Mikey, but it's cool. I like that you care enough to worry about me. But you really don't have to. I'm a big boy and can make my own decisions. Even if they are batshit crazy ones."

"I just don't like seeing someone force you to do something against your will."

"It's not like that. Fiona isn't forcing me to do nothing I don't want to do."

"So you're telling me that you would fuck a guy even if a Die Hard suckfest wasn't on offer?"

"Probably not, but that's not the only reason I'm doing it."

"What's the other reason?"

He observed me impassively before answering. "Life is about compromises. The older I get the more I realise that. And because I can see a future with Fiona, one where we live together and raise a family, I want her to know I'm capable of meeting her halfway. And if I get a fantasy or two of my own fulfilled then that's great."

My chest was suddenly tight, as if there were a band of iron around it. Gavin was even more smitten with slutty face than I thought. That didn't bode well for me. Didn't bode well at all.

"I turn thirty-seven this year and I can't believe how fast the time is flying. It feels just like yesterday I was your age, chasing after girls and living for the weekend. And I had a lot of fun, but I also think there were probably times I might have been a bit too hasty in turning things down that felt out of my comfort zone. Anyway, after your mum ran off I promised myself I'd do what I could to expand my horizons, make the most of life while I could. Have some adventures. Be it riding a motorcycle, rock climbing, sky diving, try eating sushi... and now I guess I can add fucking a dude up the ass to the list."

While most of what Gavin said made a lot of sense, I wasn't about to let him know that. "It sounds to me like you've been watching too many self-help videos on YouTube."

"Mock all you like, Grasshopper. At your age youth feels never-ending. Opportunities endless. But the sad reality is that they're not. One day you'll wake up and wonder where your abs have gone, why hangovers last longer, and you wonder why you still look tired after an eight hour sleep, and asking yourself if you'd be in a better place if you'd taken more risks when you were younger. We only have one life, Mikey, and it's best we fit as much into it as we can. Love hard and play hard. That's my new motto. Never turn down a chance to learn about yourself."

Gavin ended his guru spiel with a "Fuck this cunting thing is annoying" before slipping a hand down his pants to attack his imprisoned cock.

As comical as the sight was, I couldn't shake the gravity of his words. I also couldn't deny the very real possibility I'd be out on my ass once Fiona and her kids moved in. Sure, it wasn't going to happen overnight but I knew it would be happening sooner than later. If Gavin was willing to have sex with another man to prove his devotion then he more than liked this woman. He loved her, or was certainly on his way to doing so.

A *sort-of* stepson from a previous relationship couldn't compete with that. And it would be wrong of me to try.

Gavin was right. Sometimes you had to take a risk. Even if it put you miles outside of your comfort zone.

Chapter 14

IT WAS JUST AFTER MIDNIGHT when an incessant tap on my bedroom window alerted me to Jockey's arrival. He could have just knocked on the front door, but I'd forgotten to tell him Gavin had gone out for the night. The fact it had only been fifteen minutes since I had sent the text asking Jockey to come over suggested he must have run some of the way, no doubt keen for an answer.

He wasn't the only one keen for an answer. I had a question of my own.

I opened the window for him and he hoisted himself up inside before slithering over the window sill and onto the floor like a slinky caterpillar. He got to his feet and brushed down the front of his pants—camo ones as usual—then went and sat on my unmade bed, smiling like he was pleased to see me. "What's up, dog? I figured I wasn't gonna see you tonight. You're normally at my place by ten on Fridays."

"Sorry," I said, closing the window. "Gavin got talking when he got home from work and I lost track of the time."

"That's all good. It's the weekend now so I don't need to be in bed early."

I stood there awkwardly, wondering where I was supposed to sit. He must have sensed my indecision.

"You can sit where you like, bro. We're in your house. Not mine."

Nodding, I sat down in the office chair at my study desk. As soon as I did though, Jockey's brown eyes spotted the white envelope on the desk. His body language changed almost immediately, going from excited and casual to pensive and edgy.

"So did you read it?" he asked.

"I did. Seven times."

He chuckled. "I thought you might. It's pretty filthy, aye."

"It's very that."

He laced his hands together and leaned forward to rest his elbows on his knees, his gaze not leaving my face. "So what's the verdict? Are you gonna sign it?" He was trying his best to remain blasé about it but I could tell he was anxious.

I returned his question with one of my own, "This might sound weird but I wanted to ask you something. Do you love me?"

"Do I love you?" He frowned, taken aback.

"Yeah. Do you love me? I just need to know."

Tilting his head thoughtfully, he replied, "I care very deeply for you, Michael. As a friend. And if you sign that contract then I'll still care very deeply for you, but as my faggot. Over time it might turn into a type of love...dirty love. But not the kind you'd have with a boyfriend."

"Okay."

"That's not the answer you wanted, is it?"

I shook my head and passed him the envelope without saying anything.

He looked deflated. "I didn't think you would sign it, but I had to give it a shot, you know?"

"I understand."

"You do know I still consider you a faggot, right?"

"I know."

"That won't change. Ever. But it doesn't mean we can't stay friends."

"I think we can be more than friends, don't you?"

"Nar, bro. That might've been an option last week if you'd agreed to be the bottom, but I'm not going to fuck a faggot that turns down an offer like this. It's a pride thing. Nothing against you."

"It's just as well I signed the contract then, isn't it?"

He blinked. Once. Twice. Three times before opening the envelope to look at the last page of the contract. "You signed it!"

"I sure did."

He looked at me in disbelief. "But I thought I didn't give you the answer you wanted?"

"You didn't, but it was good enough."

Jockey couldn't wipe the smile off his face, his gaze flitting between me and my signature on the piece of paper in his hands. A signature that meant he was now the proud owner of a teenage faggot who was secretly shitting himself. There was a part of me, the cautious part still lurking in the shadows, that thought I was making a mistake. Thankfully, seeing how happy I'd just made Jockey helped suppress some of those doubts. This would be a good thing for both of us, I assured myself.

"What made you agree to sign it?" he asked.

"It just felt the right thing to do."

"Come on, Michael, you don't sign something like this just because you felt like it. You're not an idiot. You know I'm taking this contract seriously, so I expect you to as well. Now spill, why'd you sign it?"

"It's kind of embarrassing though."

"You're gonna be doing loads of embarrassing things to please me from now on, but being honest is not one of them."

"I liked the way the contract makes it sound like you'll always be there for me. Well, for as long as you decide I'm useful. I guess I feel a bit lonely at times, and...this will make me sound a bit lame but I would like some stability in my life and it feels like you're willing to give me that."

"That's nothing to be embarrassed about. It makes perfect sense. But you didn't have to sign this contract to have my loyalty. You had that already."

"But not like this." I could feel myself blushing. "When you fucked me down at the beach, I liked it. More than I thought I would. Your dick was hitting something that was driving me wild but there was something else... something that took me a while to understand."

"What was it?"

"You made me feel safe. I underestimated how fucking strong you are. I had no idea but when you pinned me down and thrusted into me I felt violated and safe in equal measure."

"You liked that?"

"Yes and no. You want me to be honest, right?"

He nodded.

"I fucking hated it. I still think I'm gonna hate it. Being reminded I'm your inferior. But I also like it for that safety reason.

The more I'm willing to accept my place beneath you the more I can find that safe place."

"Wow, bro. You're fucking deep." He saw my frown and quickly added, "But that's good. Really fucking good. I mean, works for me."

"Don't worry I also have a shallow reason."

"Which is?"

"I'm constantly horny as fuck."

He laughed. "You and me both."

"I'm so fucking horny I don't even care that I'm about to become the human equivalent of a cum sock. Just use me. It's cool. Just promise me you'll always be there."

"You have my word, Mike. I will make sure you are taken care of. I'm your alpha now. It's my job."

"Thank you, Jockey." My jaw ticked, worried I'd made a mistake already. "Shit, am I allowed to call you that anymore? Or is it sir or master?"

"Don't stress too much about that stuff just yet. You can still call me by my name. We have plenty of time to work out something more suitable. But to be honest, I'm not too hung up on that sort of shit. I'd rather you pay me respect by doing as your told."

"Okay."

"Had I known you were going to sign it, so soon, I would have put an earlier start date on the contract."

"Doesn't it start from when I sign it?"

He shook his head and pointed to small font across the bottom of the title page. "The date listed is next Friday. It felt right we commence on a Friday night, like an acknowledgement of the past two years, but I didn't put this Friday in case you needed more time to decide."

I grinned teasingly. "So technically I'm still a free man then?"

"A free faggot," he corrected. "But come next Friday you will report for duty at my house and your service begins. For real."

"For real," I echoed.

I couldn't read his face. And yet there was something crystal clear passing between us that didn't require words. We were in a grey zone between being friends and something without a name. It was both terrifying and exciting.

"Is Gavin still up?" he asked.

"He's spending the night at his girlfriend's place."

"You mean Fiona?"

My eyebrows shot up. "You know about them being together?"

"I've known for about two weeks, bro. I'm surprised you didn't tell me."

"I was going to tell you but I just worried you'd be upset."

"Pfft. Gavin's welcome to her. Fiona's a cool chick and all, and a great fuck, but I've moved on."

"Yeah. Haven't you heard? I own my own faggot now." Jockey narrowed his eyes to seductive slits. "And just between you and me, my faggot's pussy is way tighter than Fiona's. For now..."

My asshole twitched at hearing that. If I'd learned anything from reading the contract it was that I would have to accept there was no escaping ending up with a loose asshole. One of the clauses had even mentioned that Jockey's aim was to get me loose enough so he could eventually fist me. I just hoped that by the time that day came I'd be well-versed in the art of taking big things up my ass.

While I stared at his hands and imagined how painful taking one of his fists up my ass would be, Jockey began reading through the contract, checking my answers to his very personal questions. That was the reason it was so late when I had text him to come over,

I'd been busy filling in the contract for nearly three hours. Some of the questions were easy to answer, like my measurements, but others had required a level of soul searching that was downright uncomfortable. For some of them I'd had to write my answers out on the loose sheets of paper he'd provided in the envelope just to make sure I had enough space to share everything he wanted to know.

I studied his face as he read, his eyes scanning the page like a lab technician. I could sort of gauge what parts he was reading by whether he was smiling or frowning, and when he began to laugh uncontrollably I knew exactly what he'd just read.

"Aw, bro. That is fucking shameful. I didn't think anyone would be dumb enough to fall for that."

"I prefer the word naive."

Jockey shook his head, still laughing. "Nar, bro. That was just dumb. Here I was thinking I'd popped your cherry but a water pistol beat me to it."

Jockey was referring to my response to *Your most embarrassing sexual memory.*

It had happened when I was fifteen and Jockey had told Brian and I that gay dudes got off on being fucked because when the jizz went inside their ass it created what he'd described as "A super orgasm." Being the clueless idiot that I was, and a walking hard-on at the time, I was keen to experience one of these super orgasms. Rather than take a cock up my ass to find out, I began saving my cum after each wank, pouring it into an old water pistol I had found buried in the back of my closet. After a week spent collecting my semen like some sort of makeshift fertility clinic, I knew there wasn't enough jizz for my plan to work so I'd snuck into Mum and Gavin's bedroom where I found four used condoms under their bed and added Gavin's sperm with my own. When I finally did get round to shoving the water pistol up my ass and pulling the trigger, I never did get that super orgasm Jockey had told us about. All I got for my efforts was a spunk-clogged sphincter and the knowledge I had Gavin's dead swimmers inside me.

Aside from the embarrassment of Jockey now knowing my shameful secret, I had to admit that so far nothing felt too different between us. Once he was finished reading through my responses, he set the contract aside and smiled at me warmly.

"Do you have any questions for me?" he asked.

I couldn't think of any so I just shrugged.

"No questions? Fuck, if I was the one who'd just signed away ownership of my ass I'd have plenty of shit I'd wanna ask."

Worried that he might confuse my lack of questions as not having read the contract properly, I asked, "The contract says you expect me to stay over at your place at least two nights a week, I was just wondering what days they would be?"

"It'll probably change week to week. And that's two nights minimum." He glared at me to make sure I understood my commitment. "I have a high sex drive and want to make use of that pussy of yours."

"I'd expect nothing less," I replied, only half-joking.

"So if I do find a girlfriend while you're under my rule you'll still get plenty of servicing. Don't worry about that. My balls brew enough cum to service a dozen bitches."

I didn't doubt it. But I also resented it. While I was expected to remain the faithful faggot, Jockey would have the freedom to fuck who he pleased. Easing some of my resentment was knowing he'd never had much luck in the past with girls in this town, so I probably didn't have to worry too much about him sowing his wild oats.

"And you know this contract is for twelve months, right? Not a day shorter, not a day longer."

I nodded.

"If we're both still keen on doing this in a year's time then we can renew the contract. But if you want out at the end of it instead then I'll expect compensation, but I'm sure I put that in there."

He had.

If I wanted to become what the contract had referred to as "*a freerange faggot*" at the end of twelve months then I would have to pay Jockey $500. It was a lot of money but not as steep as the early termination fee, which Jockey had set at a steep two grand. And just in case I had any ideas of avoiding paying such a fee the contract made it very clear I could expect "*harsh and severe*" consequences. That should have scared me more than it did, but at this stage I could not see myself wanting to bail early. Right now I craved security and someone I could trust, and that's what becoming Jockey's faggot gave me. It also gave me access to his dick, which was also a big drawcard.

"Have you thought about where you want to get the tattoo?" he asked. "Or have you chosen the other option?"

The other option was equally disturbing: Jockey recording a video of me getting fucked at Hickford Park and then putting it online. Neither option appealed to me but I figured that was the point.

"Which one would you rather I choose?"

"I'd rather you get the tattoo," he replied. "So I'm hoping that's what you want as well."

"I wouldn't say I *want* the tattoo, but provided it's small, and somewhere sensible, then I'm not strictly opposed to getting it."

"It will be very small. It just has to say something that alludes to you being my property. And you can choose where you get it."

He reminded me of a starving cat eyeing up a bird in a tree, the need and hunger in his predatory gaze screaming *kill, kill, kill* but his body terrifyingly still, worried I might fly away in fright if he made a move too soon. It was obvious that me getting a tattoo bearing his name would be the ultimate thrill for Jockey, which I'm sure explained why he was being so reasonable about its size and placement.

"Is it okay if I have a bit more time to think about it? It's a pretty big decision either way."

"You're technically not my property for another seven days, remember? So spend the next week thinking about it, but I'll expect an answer by then when you report for duty. If you go with the tattoo option then we'll need to decide on a design and tell Darren what we want."

Jockey's words dried out my mouth and caused my stomach to flip. "You want your brother to do the tattoo?"

"Of course." He rolled up the sleeve of his shirt to show me the twisting vine over his shoulder. "He did mine so he knows what he's doing."

"And you want Darren to know about this?" I circled a finger in the air. "About us?"

"He already knows I've asked you to be my faggot. I spoke with him last week."

"Oh my God."

"Don't freak out," Jockey snapped. "Darren ain't gonna tell no one. Savage men don't nark. And they don't gossip like women."

Considering Darren was no stranger to the inside of a prison cell, I figured that was probably true. But it didn't make me feel any better knowing that Jockey's criminal older brother knew about us. "I can't believe you told him."

Jockey looked at me like I was an idiot. "I shared a room with the dude for fifteen years, Mikey. Darren and I don't have secrets. Who do you think taught me how to suck dick so good?"

"You sucked your brother off?"

"We used to suck each other off," Jockey clarified like it wasn't a big deal. "That's how I know he can keep his mouth shut...and wide open if you know what I mean."

While Jockey laughed at his own joke, I sat there picturing Jockey and Darren taking brotherly bonding a little too seriously. The image should have disgusted me and sent my ass running for the moral high ground, but it had the opposite effect. It turned me on. Turned me on a lot. Turned me on enough to almost convince me I'd made the right decision signing the contract.

"That turn you on, does it?" Jockey smirked at me. "The thought of me and Darren together?"

For a split-second I wondered if my new master was a mind reader, until I looked down and saw the swell of arousal in my jeans. "Shit," I muttered, closing my legs.

"Don't be shy, dog. If it turns you on just tell me. I won't judge you."

Without answering, I pressed down on my bulge to try and hide it.

"Oi." Jockey snapped his fingers at me. "I know you have seven days left of freedom but I'd prefer it if you didn't touch your dick in front of me. I find it quite disrespectful."

At first I thought he was joking but the look on his face was deadly serious. "Sorry."

"I know it's hard but you'll get used to that rule eventually. There are things I can do to help."

"Such as?"

"Like touching your dick for you."

"Really?" My voice cracked like I was still fourteen.

"Not right now, buddy. Maybe once the contract officially starts. And only if you're a good boy."

A compulsion gripped me and I heard myself say, "What if I wanted to be a good boy for my alpha tonight?"

Jockey looked surprised to hear what I'd just said. I was just as surprised myself.

He leaned back, an expression of triumph mixed with arousal on his face "Is my faggot offering me a free go at his pussy before the contract even starts?"

Faggot. That degrading fucking word sounded so fucking hot right now. Cruel desire throbbed every inch of my cock. I'd been longing for my second time ever since my first. I may have ditched my virginity but now I craved the experience to go with it.

I answered his demeaning question with an obedient nod.

"Fine," Jockey exhaled, sounding as if I was the one asking for a favour. And maybe I was. "If your pussy is too hungry to wait a week then go find us some lube, bitch. But be quick before I change my mind."

"Yes, sir." I don't even think I said it sarcastically.

I went into Gavin's bedroom and found a bottle of KY jelly beside his bed. I felt like such an adult knowing I was about to use the same fuck-grease my stepfather did. There was something terribly adult about it, and also something pretty pervy.

When I came back into the room, Jockey was standing up beside the bed. He had taken off his shirt and unfastened the top button of his pants. His hard cock, sticking straight upward, protruded ever so slightly from the top of his pants. I handed him the lube and he dropped his pants down around his dusty boots and began to rub the liquid all over his cock.

"How do you want me to lie?" I asked him.

"Why don't you just bend over the side of the bed," Jockey shrugged, "it'll be easier that way."

I pushed down my jeans and did as he asked. I leaned over the bed, my knees on the floor, my face pressed sideways into the covers atop the mattress. Jockey came up behind me and, with his hands, raised up my hips until they were even with his crotch. After putting some of the liquid on his middle finger, he found my asshole and stuck his finger in, lubricating me. I felt the swift, sharp sting of his ragged, dirty nail prodding my inside, and the cool feeling of the hand lotion. I elevated my asscheeks even higher for him. Jockey withdrew his finger, wiped it on the back of my t-shirt, and then moved into the area of my outstretched back thighs. His hands spread the cheeks of my ass and I felt the head of his prick, cold and slippery with the lubricant, at my opening.

The head glided smoothly in. I winced and tightened up involuntarily for a moment, then tried to relax. When he sensed that my body had rid itself of the preliminary tension, Jockey stepped in closer and the trunk of his prick, slick with the cool lube, tunnelled its way up into my insides. He was still standing up. He wrapped his arms around my waist to make sure my hips remained elevated for his convenience.

He got it all the way in, paused, inquired, "You okay?"

"Yes," I lied.

"Ready for me to start fuckin' you?"

"Ready." Another lie.

Booted feet planted solidly on the floor, crotch against my upraised butt so that I could feel the tip of his dick brushing against my lubed hole, Jockey pushed with all his strength.

"Fuck!" I cried out.

His cock went straight up inside my ass. He started in right away, stabbing and jabbing and banging me over the edge of the bed, thrusting his long, thick prick in and out of the asshole I'd given him sole ownership of.

Right at the moment I considered scrambling away and ripping up the contract, he slowed down, taking me in easy, gentle thrusts, as if the vicious thrusts had been simply to gain entry. It still hurt but the pain was manageable, easy almost.

"So you like the idea of two brothers getting it on, aye?" he asked as he rubbed my back.

"Umm...."

"You would have loved to have been a fly on the wall of our bedroom growing up." The grind of his hips became slow, deep, purposeful. "Every day when we'd get home from school we'd go to our bedroom and shut the door. Darren liked me to get naked when I did it. Then I'd slurp on that big bro meat. Licking it clean for him after he'd sweated all day at school." Jockey paused to pull me by my hair. "He liked to do what you do...fuck my face. Make sure I took that spoof in the back of my throat."

"Uh huh," I returned with a low groan.

"Too bad you're a faggot now. No more fucking my face for you."

"Yeah," I mumbled. "No more of that for me."

"I sucked Darren off for a whole year before he started to return the favour. We only had one rule. That we wouldn't try cornholing each other. Savage men don't take it up the shithole. That's for bitches like you." He slapped my ass. "Ain't that right, Mike?"

"Yeah, man." I groaned loudly as he gave my ass another slap. "Bitches like me."

He began jabbing my hole on angles, stretching my passage and loosening me up. Now I was moaning, and not at all painfully.

Jockey noticed the change in my tone. "Sounds like it's feeling pretty good now, huh? You like my dick up there?"

"Uh-huh, yeah." I said with a whimper as I pressed my ass back to meet his thrust, swallowing every inch of his rock-hard cock. My own dick had shrivelled into a little button when Jockey first forced himself in, but now it was starting to lengthen and throb. My breathing slowed and deepened, as I felt myself relax and accept what was happening. It wasn't as enjoyable as that night down at the beach, but maybe it was because I didn't have any alcohol or drugs in my system. Still, I knew I'd get used to this and it was good, mostly.

"Push back. Take it. Be the slut you always wanted to be." He stuffed a thumb in my mouth and I groaned again, slurping on it and mewling as I pushed back against his rod.

With his other hand, Jockey tightened his grip on my waist and began to fuck harder. "You were born for this, Mike. Born to be a faggot." He picked up speed and started getting rough. "This is you surrendering your hole forever, bitch. Your manhood. You're going to be possessed, fucked and owned."

"That's what I want," I groaned. "Take it all, Jockey. It's yours."

"Fucking slut," came the reply.

My face was burning, my ass was on fire, my cock so hard I thought I was going to start shooting.

My sphincter was stretched beyond imagination, tighter than a guitar string, but playing sweet, high-pitched fuck-music. His dick burrowed deeper and deeper, into areas never touched before, I felt the sweat from his chest on my back, and I pressed my face into the mattress, tamed and enslaved.

Jockey kept calling me names—he had an authority complex. Making sure I knew he as the man and I was the bitch. He called me that: "bitch," "pussy," "cunt," "slut," "whore," "faggot," and everything else he could think of. He humiliated me, but not enough that I wanted him to stop. Jockey's magnificent cock was battering me into a new person.

I heard my helpless whimpers echoing through the room, experiencing the sensation of being owned by another human being.

The closer he got to his orgasm, the stranger his dialogue got. "Get ready bitch. I've been saving this faggot fuel up for days," he said between grunts. I would have laughed if I hadn't been so absorbed with what was happening inside my ass. The only thing missing was some cheesy porn music.

I loved the feeling of his balls slapping against my ass in the frenzied motions, the way his hardness glided up the path it had cut out for itself, the way the thick, obstinate head of his cock felt when it touched that deepest, innermost part of me.

Jockey pounded in and out of me, fucking me thoroughly, deeply, totally, the way he would have fucked a woman whose opening had long been stretched to receive his generous girth. The engorged shaft filled me, drove its way deep into me. It was something not to be stopped, no matter how deeply it went, no matter how unready for it I was. It found its own path, ripping aside all that was in its way, invincible.

Within a matter of minutes I felt his hard flesh widening even more, pulsating inside me in the familiar way before orgasm and, with one last furious thrust, so abrupt and penetrating that it made me cry out a little with pain, Jockey's cock exploded inside me, the warm semen gushing through me like a rampaging river, and he collapsed on my back and we lay across the bed, our bodies joined, until he was completely drained of his excessive alpha male juices.

"Was that good?" I asked from under his weight.

"Fuck yeah. I've been fucking needing that." After another breath, he said, "For, like, a while."

Turning my face for a kiss I did not receive; I couldn't help but think *so have I.*

∞

About the Author

ZANE LIVES IN NEW ZEALAND in a rundown pink shack near the beach with his gaming-obsessed flatmate and a demanding cat. He is a fan of ghost stories, road trips, and nights out that usually lead to his head hanging in a bucket the next morning.

He enjoys creating characters who have flaws, crazy thoughts and a tendency to make bad decisions. His stories are steamy, unpredictable and tend to explore the darker edge of desire.

Milton Keynes UK
Ingram Content Group UK Ltd.
UKHW010948061123
432055UK00008B/355

9 798223 739227